To my family.
— M.L.W.

Published by Creston Books, LLC in Berkeley, California.
www.crestonbooks.co

CIP data for this book is available from the Library of Congress.

Type set in Feast of Flesh by Blambot and Plantagenet Cherokee.
Source of Production: Worzalla Books, Stevens Point, Wisconsin
Printed and bound in the United States of America
1 2 3 4 5

JACK DEATH

M.L. WINDSOR

Creston Books

JACK DEATH

M.L. WINDSOR

CHAPTER 1

In a town not much different from your own there lived a little boy of unusual parentage.

His mother was normal. Her name was Dorothy, and she had bushy brown hair and a predilection for shortbread biscuits, the world's most disgusting cookie.

But back to the boy.

His name was Jefferson, but he was called Jack. Probably because no young boy wishes to be called Jefferson. I do not, however, know why he did not simply go by "Jeff."

Jack was short and dark-haired and green-eyed and terrible at sports. There is nothing so horrible at being bad at sports when you are Jack's age. But he was, and that was that. Luckily, Jack was also clever, and fast, and just as good at getting out of trouble as he was at getting into it.

You see, Jack had a very unusual father, who was also clever, and fast, and just as good as getting out of trouble as he was at getting into it.

His father was Death.

Death, coincidentally, is very bad at football.

You probably think Jack knew nothing of his heritage, and would grow up, have an adventure, and realize (gasp!) at the end who his father really was.

Well, you're wrong.

Jack knew. It was The Secret, the one he couldn't tell anybody. Not even his best friend Booger, not that he would. Booger was worse than a girl at keeping a Secret.

Everybody has a Secret, whether it's an ogre on your mother's side or a dimwit troll for a second cousin. It happens to the best of families. But Death does not make many appearances on family trees. He is very busy, you know.

And Jack would have kept The Secret, probably for a very, very long time, except that one day, his best friend Booger was killed.

CHAPTER 2

Let's begin. Not at the beginning, if you please, but close enough for comfort. Jack and Booger were riding the bus to school down a long, gray, winding lane. It was raining (it usually was), and the bus was just coming around the best curve of the ride.

All of the children quieted down for the curve, waiting for the violent jerk that the bus driver would make, sending them careening to the right as the bus's left set of wheels lifted clear off the ground and the kids on the right side got a view down the ravine.

It was all great fun.

Booger and Jack had managed to get a seat on the right side today, because the kid before Jack's stop had been sick. They looked excitedly out the window, waiting for the deathly view. Once, some of the older

3

kids said, the bus's wheels had gone over the curb, and all of the children had had to run to the left to keep the bus from plummeting down the canyon.

Booger said they were lying. Jack said he was a spoilsport.

They were just about to round the bend.

"Here we go!" said Booger, who couldn't help but narrate his own life, an affliction that curses the best of us. Jack was silent. He had the window seat, and he felt his heart go *da-dum, da-dum, da-dum* as the bus turned...

HONK.

Did you think that was the bus's horn? It wasn't. It was Urkel Underbottom, blowing a sports horn right in Booger's ear.

Maybe you have met a bully or two in your life, but I assure you that you have never met one quite so mean, quite so nasty, quite so smug as Urkel Underbottom. One would think with a name like that, he would have been a poor little child in glasses, with knobby knees and a shrimpy stature. Oh, if only he had been! But Urkel Underbottom was not.

Urkel was mean.

Urkel was large.

Urkel had bat ears and a pig nose and gorilla arms, and he was strong as a bear and mean as a hippo (if you have never met a hippo, then consider yourself lucky). He always wore a dark shirt with pizza and oatmeal stains, not because his mother could not afford to wash them, but because he hated the scent of fresh detergent, and once wrestled his mother when she tried to take his dirty clothes hamper away in the night. He won, barely.

You probably think this bully had some redeeming quality, like a love for cats. He did not. He hated cats.

Some of Urkel's favorite tricks included: holding boys' heads in the toilet as he flushed, hanging boys by their belt loops on hooks in the utility closet, and supergluing boys' heads together during class.

He was not as good at picking on girls, however. That required a lot of words and a clever tongue, neither of which Urkel had.

And Urkel's favorite victim was—yes, you've guessed it already. Booger Reynolds.

How do you think Booger got the name Booger? Do you think he liked that nickname? Do you think his mother gave him that name in a burst of postpartum affection? No, what happened was—

Well.

Let's focus on the present. Urkel honked the horn again, right in Booger's ear. Some of the children laughed, hoping Urkel would like them and not pick on them. Some of them frowned and looked away, hoping Urkel would not see them and not pick on them. Some of them told him to quiet down, hoping Urkel would just shut up.

"Leave him alone, Urkel," said Jack.

Booger whimpered and shook his pale head, his white curls bouncing with the motion. His hands were clamped over his ears, but the damage had already been done.

"Leave him alone, Urkel," Urkel mocked. HONK.

The bus had already made the big turn, and Jack had missed it. He was frustrated, he was annoyed, he was exasperated at this big armadillo-faced enemy beside them. He swiped for the horn, but Urkel held it higher. HONK.

Jack leaned over Booger, who was still whimpering. Before Urkel could understand what was happening, Jack unclipped Urkel's belt buckle and yanked off his belt.

Many things happened at once.

Urkel's pants fell down, revealing a pair of bright red boxers with white unicorns on them.

Booger let out a shriek of horror.

Urkel frantically tried to pull up his jeans, even as the other children roared with laughter.

Jack grabbed the horn. He turned it around so it faced his tormentor.

HONK.

With a yelp, Urkel stumbled backwards and into the opposite row of seats. The pair of girls sitting there let out a frightened, hysterical cry, mingled with laughter, as they scrambled to get away from Urkel's bare knees and unicorn-patterned bottom.

Urkel's face turned very, very red.

"I'm going to kill you, Jack Hallows," he growled.

And that was the start of that.

CHAPTER 3

Did you think that was where Booger died? I'm sorry to say it is not. Sorry because it would have been much more pleasant for Booger to die among friends.

But don't worry. We're coming to that part.

The school bus arrived at school. It was still raining, and the children leapt off the curb and ran for the glass double doors. Urkel came last, plotting.

Jack did not worry too much about Urkel's threat. It was, after all, the seventh one he had received that year from Urkel (though he had stopped officially counting after the fourth). He went off to math class and learned about fractions.

Meanwhile, one of Death's Reapers sharpened his scythe.

A scythe is basically a long, curved, sharp blade,

in case you are wondering. See the picture below.

Booger and Jack had almost all of their classes together, which is why they had become friends. They were also both terrible at sports. Booger was big, but his eyesight was horrible. The gym teacher would call Booger a mole and laugh. Jack would throw dodge-balls at his gym teacher and blame his bad aim.

At lunchtime, Urkel came for Jack.

It might be helpful to know that Urkel had a great deal of troll blood in him. Not only was his great-grandfather a troll, but also his half-uncle and his cousin's cousins. The women in his family had a weakness for trolls.

Not that Urkel knew this. If he had, he might even have been proud of it. Who knows. But certainly he walked and stomped and stalked like a troll, as he blundered his way over to where Jack was sitting with Booger in a back corner of the lunchroom.

Booger shook Jack's shoulder. Jack turned

around and—

SMACK!

Cherry pie, right in Jack's face.

The lunchroom howled with laughter. Urkel broke into a wide, ugly grin.

Death's Reaper, unnoticed, stepped into the lunchroom.

Jack wiped his eyes to remove cherry gunk and pie crust.

"Jack," said Booger, a warning.

Jack stood up and threw his lasagna into Urkel's laughing face.

"Run!" Jack cried, as Urkel recovered from his sputtering and growled, low and deep. Because there comes a time in every hero's life where the best course of action is to flee, flee, flee.

Thunder crashed outside. It was, you might say, an omen.

Urkel shoved the table into Jack and Booger. Jack stumbled, but Booger fell to the floor with a crash. Jack didn't see Booger fall—he was too busy sprinting away, brushing right past the Reaper on his way.

He didn't see him, but he shuddered.

Urkel considered chasing Jack, but years of experience had taught him just how exhausting and ineffective that could be. In all his time, he had only caught Jack once. Instead, Urkel turned toward Booger.

Poor, fallen Booger.

I don't really want to tell this part. A boy's death is his own business, don't you think? It is a little, *voyeuristic,* if you will, to watch Booger as he struggled to rise, his chest heaving, his breath coming out in little spurts. He was very, very afraid of Urkel, especially without Jack around to defend him. At some point, Jack did turn around, and did see that his friend had not followed. But Booger did not know this. He did not know that Jack was coming back for him.

Urkel reached for Booger, wiping lasagna sauce from his cheeks.

And that was when the window to the lunchroom shattered. In came a troll, who gobbled up Booger in three large bites.

I'm sorry, was that unexpected?

I assure you, it was for Booger, too. Up until then, he had only spotted trolls far off in the hills on the bus ride to school, prancing around in the wild reserves where they were allowed to run free. There had not been a troll break for decades now. The fences were very tall.

The Reaper moved quickly, snatching up Booger's poor young soul. It took him away from the lunchroom. Even the Reaper wished a little bit that the troll had been hungry for Urkel, not Booger.

But the troll had eaten Booger, and that was that.

CHAPTER 4

The lunch ladies trapped the troll in a giant mashed potato pot. The children were all sent home early. The school had to meet with lawyers to figure out how not to be sued. The janitors went into the lunchroom to clean up the remains of Booger. Finally, Magical Creature Control showed up and wrapped the troll in chains to take him back to the reserve. The school's mashed potatoes would not taste the same for months.

"We'll get the bones out, one way or another," Magical Creature Control assured Booger's mother, who swooned. "We'll return them to you in a very nice box."

Booger's mother was not comforted.

"Mom, it was Booger!" Jack burst out, as he

hopped inside her minivan. Dorothy sighed.

"I wish it could have been Urkel," she muttered.

"What?"

"Nothing, dear. The troll ate Booger?"

It did, and I wish this story could be about Jack's heroic rescue of Booger from the hands of Death. It is not, though. You see, Grim Reapers are strong and fast and quick with their work, and once one has you in his well-manicured hands, you are well and truly gone.

Dorothy drove Jack back home. They lived in a gingerbread neighborhood—that is to say, a neighborhood where every house was cute and small and much the same. It might sound fun. It might even sound delicious. But really it was just rather boring.

"I'm going to go play," Jack said, as Dorothy cooked dinner. Beep, beep went the microwave.

"Don't stay out too long!"

Jack left, not to rescue the poor, troll-eaten Booger (may he rest in peace), but to form a plan. Plans are very useful when you are in trouble. Jack, you see, was in quite a lot of trouble. The problem was, he did not realize just how much. Not yet.

Jack went down the lane, passing rose gardens and neatly clipped hedges, yapping little dogs, and overly friendly neighbors, until finally he came to the pond at the back of the gingerbread neighborhood. He remembered how he and Booger had played pirates on the pond, and for a moment Jack thought he might do something forbidden to boys and cry.

"What are you doing?"

Jack looked up and scowled. It was Nadine Jang.

Nadine Jang had been Jack's neighbor for as long as he could remember. She had long, dark, silky hair that curled just around her shoulders and dark, wide, big eyes that were just above her cheeks. Nadine was nice, Nadine was smart, Nadine was everything you could ever want in a friend, except for one thing: her father was the strictest man in the world.

Oh, you don't believe me. You think, why, Nadine's wandering around the pond by herself! Her father is not so bad after all. Well, if you'd stop interrupting, I will explain it to you.

Nadine's father, Gregory Jang, was the strictest, most rigid, most nervous parent in the history of all parents. He worried about burglars and bedbugs at night. He worried about carbon monoxide and burnt toast in the mornings. He worried that Nadine's homework was not neat enough on the way to school (he knew all about the bus's most fun turn, and strictly disapproved), or that fire-breathing ninjas would abduct her during classes.

It is not very fun having a father like Gregory. You will probably be safe, but all of your classmates will wonder why you can't go to any sleepovers or playdates or field trips. They will be confused as to why you eat your lunch alone in an allergen-free room and why, on days when you have gym class, you are required to wear a helmet at all times. On the other hand, the aluminum foil that your father ties around your backpack straps significantly reduces your chances of alien abduction.

But there were no aliens around at that moment. Instead, Nadine was staring at Jack, who was staring back at Nadine, wondering where her very strict father was.

"He's away on business," Nadine said, reading his mind. "I have a babysitter." For Nadine, those were the most exciting days of her life.

"Well, go away. I'm busy."

"I'm sorry about Booger."

"I'm fine!" Jack said. "It's just something in my eye. I'm allergic to pond water."

Nadine kindly pretended to examine some of the water lilies.

When Jack had gotten control of his allergies, he said, "I think it was murder."

"It was. The troll murdered Booger. It ate him, too."

"Not the troll."

"Not the troll?"

Jack shook his head. "The person who let the

troll out. He murdered Booger."

Nadine was quiet. She knew, just as well as Jack, that the person who managed the troll fence on the reserve was Ubork Underbottom, Urkel's father.

"It could have been an accident," Nadine said. Behind them, the pond rippled as a pond monster swam beneath the surface. It was doing laps, because its wife had told it recently that it was putting on a few pounds.

"Muscle," the pond monster had replied.

"You haven't moved in centuries," his wife had huffed. "The only muscle you ever use is your tongue."

"Well, I'd prefer you use that one a little less," the pond monster retorted. But he was very vain and so started swimming laps anyway.

But I digress again.

"I'm going to find out," Jack said. He hadn't yet worked out his plan, but it was helpful to say it out loud. It helped steel his resolve. "I'm going to go over to the reserve and find out what happened."

"How? By asking Mr. Underbottom?"

"I'll conduct an investigation."

Nadine looked dubious.

"If you conduct an investigation," she said, "you will need clues. And suspects. And leads."

"Yes," said Jack haughtily. "So?"

Nadine scuffed her shoe in the dirt. She had

read a great many mystery stories, stuck at home as her father prattled on about air pollution and contagious diseases and suspicious neighbors. One day, she thought, she would be a detective like Mr. Holmes, Family Secret or not.

Oh, yes. Nadine's family had a Secret, too. But we are not there yet.

"I could help," Nadine offered.

The horror! Jack tried not to gape. A girl, help him on his adventure? She would ruin just about everything.

"I don't need any help," Jack said. "But thank you anyway." And he pushed past her and ran home.

CHAPTER 5

Investigations are generally most successful after dark. It is because all of the lies and Secrets, under the cover of night, feel it is safer to crawl and creep and slither out, and if you are very careful and very quiet, you may just be able to catch a few.

Jack knew this well, and so he waited until the sun had gone down and the moon had risen before tiptoeing out of his house and into the night.

The world looked different in the dark: all the colors had been stripped away, and all the noises vibrated deep down in Jack's heart. The air had a prickly quality, and a hundred pairs of unseen eyes watched as he loped across his street and up his lane and onto the main road.

It was not all that far to the troll reserve, but it

was far enough that Jack wished more than once he had brought a coat, or that Booger was still around. Booger hated sneaking about in the night, but usually Jack could bribe him with food or the promise of food. Booger was not fat, mind you, just hungry. I know that's what you were thinking, and it is disrespectful of poor, fallen Booger.

Jack had just turned onto the last stretch, leading up to the gates of the troll reserve, when he heard a whisper.

Jackkkk.

Jackkkkkkkk.

Jack hurried on. It could have just been the branches of the trees above him, creaking and swishing in the wind. It could have just been the rustle of the leaves below, skirting across the empty road. It could have—

Jackkkkkkkkkkkkkkkkk!

Jack broke into a run. The whisper seemed to gain in volume, to rush to follow him.

Jack! Jackk! Jackkk!

He tripped over a root and went sprawling into the mud, ruining the front of his pajamas. Jack gasped, scrambling to twist around and free his foot. A figure approached, cloaked in darkness.

"Jack," the figure whispered. It loomed over him.

"Nadine!"

Nadine pushed back the hood of her coat (some-one, at least, had been sensible enough to wear one) and smiled shyly. "I saw you leave," she said. "I thought you might be going on an investigation."

"Does your dad know you're out?"

"No, he's away, remember?"

Jack scowled. He did not want Nadine to see how much she had frightened him, so he straightened up and said, puffing out his chest, "I don't need your help."

"Oh!" Nadine looked down and scuffed her sneaker against the muddy road. "I just thought, maybe, with Booger gone..."

She didn't want to finish the statement and reveal to Jack that she desperately hoped they might become friends. Sometimes, when she was alone in her room, with her dehumidifier and humidifier on opposite corners of her desk, antibacterial soap in an industrial-sized dispenser on her windowsill (next to the air filter and the carbon monoxide detector), she would make lists of all the people from school she might be friends with. Each one was given a "pro" and a "con" column, and then ranked in order of Most Likely To Be a Good Friend.

Jack was somewhere near the bottom, but he was also her closest neighbor. And Nadine had to start somewhere.

"I brought an extra jacket," Nadine said, handing him the bunched up ball she was holding. The jacket was pink and blue, a girl's coat, but Jack shrugged it on anyway. "I know all about investigations. I've read all of the Sherlock Holmes and Sammy Keyes books and—"

"Fine, then," Jack said. "But we have to be quiet. We're almost at the gate."

Nadine nodded solemnly.

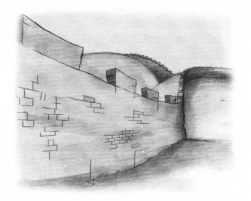

CHAPTER 6

If you have never been by a troll fence, allow me to describe this one to you.

It was tall. It was black. It was strong and thick and made of concrete and bones. On top there were coils of barbed wire which, every other day, were electrified. There were no doors in the troll fence, because you would not want to go in just as much as you would not want anything to come out.

There was, however, one gate.

The gate was where the guards stayed. Presumably, the guards made sure that the tall, thick, black concrete wall remained as tall and thick as ever. Escaped trolls were good for no one. Except perhaps trolls, but not many people cared about them.

The head guard, as I have said, was Ubork

Underbottom. Ubork was also tall and thick and made partly of bone, but he was a pasty white and did not have a lick of concrete in him. He smelled like a thousand garlic bulbs mashed together with microwaved fish.

Have you ever smelled microwaved fish? Coincidentally, it is the only smell that will rid a house of a poltergeist, because even they have the sense to detest it.

But I digress.

Ubork Underbottom was on watch that night. He was already very cranky, as he had gotten an earful from Magical Creature Control.

"There is no hole in the fence!" Ubork had shouted at them.

"Then the troll must have come through the gate!" they shouted back.

"How is that my fault?" he had roared.

"Because you're supposed to be guarding it!" they howled.

The entire episode was very upsetting, and Ubork had settled into his night watch with a jam and ham sandwich and a long list of employees he could fire (along with a longer list of employees he could threaten to fire). Someone had made Ubork look stupid, and if there was one thing Ubork would not tolerate, it was other people realizing he was not as smart as he pretended to be.

Up crept Nadine and Jack, keeping close to the wall of the troll reserve. They did not know that Magical Creature Control had already searched the perimeter and found no opening, so they were wasting time finding out the same exact thing on their own. Unfortunately, this is often the case with amateur sleuths.

"Well," Nadine said with a yawn, after they had walked almost a mile along the wall. "I guess the troll must have gone through the gate."

"But that means someone let him out," Jack said.

"Who would do that?"

Just then, a voice cut through the darkness:
"WHO'S THERE?"

It was Ubork's voice, and it was followed by a bright yellow searchlight that swung toward the children. With a cry, Nadine flung her hands up to shield her eyes, and Jack dove sideways. He grabbed Nadine's elbow and pulled, and the two sprinted down the hill and away from the troll gate. The searchlight moved up and down, up and down, arcing closer to them and then away.

"Well," Nadine said, as they paused by the road, gasping for breath. "I suppose that was a dead end."

Jack was about to reply when a dark car pulled up. This is, shall we say, where things got interesting.

CHAPTER 7

Persimmon York was the type of man who had been very little liked as a child. This affected his entire life thereafter: he was always trying to prove, whether with money or a new suit or a disgustingly oily new haircut, that he was a Very Likable Fellow. Such men, you will find, can be very dangerous indeed, especially when they have at least an ounce of cleverness to go with their ego.

"Hello, Ubork!" he called, as he drove up in his long black car. He was wearing his suit from the office, along with a wolf mask that concealed his face and his oily new haircut. "How are you this fine evening?"

Ubork grunted. Persimmon did not like Ubork because Ubork did not like him, but Persimmon comforted himself that Ubork was fat and old and much less well-paid. After all, it was very easy to be jealous of a man in Persimmon's position. Such authority! Such power! Such wealth!

Well, compared to Ubork, at least.

"Someone's been creeping about," Ubork snarled, his pimply face poking out from the guard tower.

Persimmon gave a little tinkling laugh—*heHE-he, heHehe*—and said, "Spooked a little after today, Ubork?" He had heard that the man's disgusting little child had been roaming about in the same lunchroom as the troll and thought it would have been great fun if the troll had chosen Urkel for his lunch. That would have wiped the sneer right off Ubork's face.

"Someone might be watching," Ubork said stubbornly. "Maybe the government."

HeHEhe, heHEhe, heHEhe went Persimmon's laugh. He had a bit of garden gnome in him, generations back, and if you have ever heard a garden gnome laugh, you will know just how grating this noise could be. Ubork winced.

"We have our own men in the government, my dear Ubork," Persimmon said when he had recovered himself. He wanted to linger a few minutes longer, as he did love a good laugh at someone else's expense. But there was business to attend to. "Open the gate! I need to make a delivery."

Screeeeeech went the gate. Beyond, trolls howled and ogres roared. A few garden gnomes even laughed. Persimmon suppressed a shiver, reminding himself that in his Model X7 luxury car, he was entirely safe. Or so the Boss claimed.

The two children who slipped in after him, however, had no such guarantee.

CHAPTER 8

Oh, why would they do that, you ask? It was dangerous, it was foolish, it was impromptu! I wish I could tell you. More than that, I wish I could say that I was just playing a trick, and that in fact the two children went straight home to bed and forgot all about this nastiness. It would make for a much shorter story.

But no, Nadine and Jack had locked eyes and, without any further discussion, ran after the big dark car as it lumbered through the gates of the reserve. If there was any way to learn more about the mystery, it was by following this stranger, who was entering forbidden grounds with the help of Ubork Underbottom, the supposed guard. Why anyone would want to go into the reserve was beyond the pair, but like good detectives, they intended to find out.

Of course, you cannot chase a car on foot. You will only end up looking like a fool, your arms flapping wildly as you shake your umbrella at the fleeing vehicle, rubble shooting up at you from the tires as you wipe your sweating forehead in the hot August sun, thinking to yourself that you should never have accepted an assignment in *Greece,* and if you had, you should never have bothered to bring your old umbrella—

But the children.

Well, they stopped running almost as soon as they passed through the gate, and though Ubork was watching closely to make sure no creatures ran *out* of the reserve, he was not expecting to see any creatures run *into* it. Thus, he missed the two dark shapes entirely. You see, most of the time, people only see what they expect to. It is a very sad fact of my existence.

Screeeeeeeech. The gate shut behind them. The two children were now alone in the reserve in the dark, the car rumbling up the dirt road of the hill usually meant for construction trucks.

"Well," Nadine whispered, "what now?"

Jack had been thinking the same thing. But this was his adventure, he thought to himself, and his plan, and so he pointed imperiously up the hill where the car had disappeared.

"We follow it," he said.

"But it might be miles and miles."

"You can go home if you wish."

A troll roared from somewhere within the reserve. In fact, it was laughing at a very funny joke that its sister-in-law had just made, but the children had no way of knowing this and thought the noise could just as well have been a hungry howl. Trolls are always hungry.

"If you want to," Jack said, trembling. "It's okay. I shouldn't have brought a girl in here anyway." He was thinking that he could offer to walk her back, and thus excuse his cowardice through his gentlemanliness.

"No," said Nadine, who after making her first friend was keen not to disappoint him. "I want to keep going. Follow the car."

"Follow the car," Jack repeated faintly.

The hill grew steeper and steeper as Nadine and Jack climbed. Their legs burned, their hearts pattered, their breath whooshed in and out. Soon it felt as though they were walking up a wall, and Nadine and Jack had to use their hands to help them climb, wondering all the while how the car had managed the slope (it had four-wheel drive).

"Is it much farther?" Nadine asked.

"Can't be," Jack replied.

But it was. Up and up the children went, not

daring to rest with all the sounds of the creatures around them. Luckily almost everything hungry and dangerous was asleep, and the most that the children ran into were a few Welsh fairies who tried to steal Nadine's hair before Jack swatted them away. Which was unfortunate, because her hair would have made a very nice addition to their fairy nest.

After miles and miles of such torture, Jack finally spotted a house on the top of the hill. And next to it, parked haphazardly by the front door, was the large black car.

Nadine and Jack tiptoed close to the orange-lit window. Both of them were having second thoughts, but they wanted to seem brave, and besides, they had just climbed a very tall, very steep hill.

I wish I could skip this next part.

But if you are here, I suppose you deserve to know, just like Nadine and Jack, who had climbed all that way.

You see, another Grim Reaper rounded the corner of the house. It tried the back door first, and then a window, and upon finding both of these locked, walked right in through the front door (its last resort, and a rather unpleasant one, was to walk straight through the wall).

Inside, Persimmon York had taken off his wolf mask, to reveal his pasty, pimply, snub-nosed face.

"That is a ridiculous haircut," a man said, from the shadowy depths of an old and bulbous armchair. The window near Nadine and Jack was open a few inches, and they could hear everything.

Persimmon blushed. "It was very expensive."

"You *are* a fool, aren't you?"

"It's quite in fashion," Persimmon huffed.

The children leaned closer to get a view of the man in shadow, almost pressing their noses up against the glass. Inside, the room looked like something you might find in a castle, all bear rugs and stone walls and large fireplaces. The man in shadow was a great beast of a fellow, his dark outline showing him to be similar in shape to an overgrown toad with a lemon of a head squashed onto its neck.

The man in shadow had apparently said something else, for Persimmon began to answer.

"It's just not something that can happen *all at once,* you see."

"And why not?"

"Why? Well, they would suspect it, for one. But a little here, a little there...no one will see it coming. See *your* plan coming."

"Why do we *not* want them to see it coming?"

Persimmon looked honestly flummoxed. He tugged on his collar, he wrung his hands, he stroked back his oily hair. "Because it's Secret."

"It WAS Secret," said the man in shadow. "Bears and broomsticks! Can anyone carry out an evil plot properly?"

Nadine and Jack glanced at one another. So poor Booger's death was not just an unfortunate accident. It was part of some larger evil plan.

"I followed your directions exactly," protested Persimmon, rubbing his buggy eyes.

"Yes, but where is the initiative! The creativity! The innovation!" The shadow man threw his arms up at each of these sentences, punctuating them with what looked like a cheerleading move. "Didn't I say in the interview that I didn't want minions, I wanted protégés?"

"As evil as myself and just a little less brilliant," Persimmon quoted.

"Precisely!' Another toss of his arms. "And what did I get? You! This!"

"I can let all the creatures out, if you wish," said Persimmon huffily. Nadine gasped, and the two children ducked down from the window. Let all the creatures out? Why, that would be madness! That would be chaos!

"Did you hear something?" asked the shadow man.

"If you would like me to take the *initiative* to find out," said Persimmon, sulking, "I could—"

"That! Did you see that?"

The children crouched closer to the wall of the house, shivering and wide-eyed, sure they would be caught and then fed to the ugliest troll—which, indeed, would have been their fate, except that the man in shadow had not spotted them. He had actually caught a glimpse of the Reaper as it moved forward and sat itself down on another armchair, but the Reaper touched up its invisibility spell and leaned back, kicking its legs up on the coffee table.

"Never mind. It's gone."

"So would you like me to open the gates?"

"No, Percy, I would not."

Persimmon cringed; he hated that nickname, mostly since bullies had spun it into a rhyme they chanted when they attacked him—*No Mercy for Percy! No Mercy for Percy!*

"In fact, there is very little left that I need you to do."

Persimmon breathed a sigh of relief, and was just starting to think of what type of holiday he would like to go on when the ogre burst in.

CHAPTER 9

Do you know what it's like to be surprised by an ogre? Especially when you are dreaming of white sands and fruity drinks sipped out of coconut shells with bendy straws? Well, Persimmon did, though blissfully, the feeling did not last long. The ogre sprung upon him and gobbled him up in four quick bites.

"Heel!" said the man in shadow sharply.

The ogre, which was a well-trained brute by the name of Frank, made a face. Persimmon was not very pleasant to eat and ogres, unlike trolls, generally prefer a less bony meal.

"Get me the telephone," said the man in shadow, and Frank the ogre obediently retrieved it.

A tamed ogre, you say! That stretches credibility. But so it was. If you must know, Frank and the man in shadow had been raised as foster brothers of a sort. But that is rather more than nosy minds need to know.

"Here, have some antacids," said the man in shadow irritably, as Frank the ogre began to gag. "And go in the other room. I'm making an important call."

Nadine and Jack shivered below the sill, not daring to look back in. If they had, they might have spotted the Reaper making off with Persimmon's poor soul (the fool of a Reaper had let his invisibility slip again, though luckily the man in shadow was too pre-occupied to notice).

"We should go," Nadine whispered, and Jack tried not to look too relieved. But just then they heard the stomping footsteps of the ogre as it marched out-side and let out a great, long belch.

"Yes, hello?" said the shadow man from inside. His voice took on a new quality, as if he had swallowed a frog. In fact, the man was trying very hard to make his voice sound deeper, which he believed made him sound more important. "Mmhmm," he said, at various intervals. Jack and Nadine remained frozen in place, looking at where the ogre was now fanning his face with a gossip magazine.

"Of course I remembered, Your Excellency. When has your trusted Crusty forgotten anything?" A pause. "Well, besides that." Another pause. "And that." Another pause. "Yes, well, people change, and I assure you, I did not forget about tonight. In *fact*"—he drew out the word, savoring it on his tongue—"I am here in the reserve right now! Yes, Frank is with me."

Frank the ogre let out another belch, and patted himself on the chest.

"Well," said the man Crusty, sounding pleased with himself, "it is the largest reserve in the country—hold on, I have a brochure—'by density, not square acres.' And the release is all set and ready to go."

Release? Nadine mouthed to Jack. He just shook his head and looked quickly back to where the ogre was now smoking a cigar by the door.

"Oh, yes," said Crusty solemnly. "Plenty of the proper bloodlines in town, like the Underbottoms. Three generations of trolls in the past seven of their family. A little ogre blood, too. And then there are the Coltbloods, and the Sweeneys, and the Pickleplums, and—yes, yes. Plenty of support for the cause."

Jack shivered. Frank the ogre had shuffled off again, back inside the house, but his presence had brought home to Jack just how vulnerable they were, trapped in the middle of the reserve of Magical Creatures.

"Oh, yes," Crusty said again, his voice softening. "We will get them, Your Excellency. The little Nadine will be the first to go."

Nonsense, nonsense, nonsense, the children heard. And then—Nadine's name was mentioned.

She looked shocked, and then frightened, and then worried, while Jack looked at her sideways and wondered just how his overprotected neighbor could be mixed up in such nonsense.

Nadine did not know, but she had a good guess: it had to do with her own family Secret.

"We'll get her," purred Crusty. "And all the rest of the Unfortunates."

Unfortunates. Jack had heard that word before, mostly from adults, mostly in hushed tones when they didn't think Jack was listening. He had asked his mother once what it meant, and after scolding him until she was red in the face for saying it, she explained that "Unfortunates" were people with Magical Creature blood in them.

"But that's basically everybody," Jack had protested. "Including me."

"Hush your mouth. How many times do I have to tell you not to talk about that? Now, be a dear and go fetch my shortbread cookies."

Leaning against the house wall, Nadine looked just as pale as Jack felt. Maybe she was just like him. Maybe someone special—maybe even Death—was her father, too.

Could he and Nadine Jang be brother and sister? Gross.

But Jack didn't have time to ruminate on this

unsavory possibility. For it is then that Crusty hung up the phone and shouted to Frank, "Open the gates!"

CHAPTER 10

But! you say, *how was it that Crusty hated Unfortunates when he was practically foster brothers with an ogre?*

But! you say, *what did Crusty mean by "proper bloodlines" like the Underbottoms?*

But! you say, *how was it that Crusty was able to open the gate when he was high up on a hill?*

Well, you are in luck. I will answer all of these questions, starting with the last.

It was a button.

Not a small red button, but a big white one hooked up to the inside of the little house. Frank the ogre ambled over and pressed it with one of his fat, smoke-stained fingers.

The hill began to rumble. At first, Jack wasn't sure he was hearing properly, but one look at Nadine's face confirmed it. "The gates," she whispered. "He's opening all of them."

"But there's only one—"

KAPOW!

The deafening explosion surrounded them. Nadine moved closer to Jack and Jack moved closer to Nadine, and if they had been just a year or two younger, they might have cried. For in the pale moonlight they could clearly see the damage the explosion had caused:

The high wall surrounding the reserve had been blown to bits.

Frank the ogre made a few unpleasant, guttural noises from inside. Jack and Nadine dared to pop their heads over the sill once more.

"Well, Frank," said Crusty. He was still in shadow, with his great toad body and his squashed lemon head outlined in the darkness. "I suppose we can't be sure that the creatures will know the difference, but there are often casualties in a war, after all."

Frank the ogre made a few more noises. He was waving his heavy gray arms, occasionally rubbing his bald head with one of them.

"Oh, but you can sniff out the blood, can't you?

Go on, try it. I have a little giant, a little troll, and a good dollop of satyr in me. Do you smell that? Sweet as cherry pie."

Frank the ogre gave a great sniff and then a thumbs up.

"But the others...oh, they smell terrible! Mermaid lines smell like a filthy ocean; elf lines smell like a dusty shoe; fairy lines smell like a sour apple lollipop—"

Frank the ogre rather rudely interrupted here, raising his voice urgently.

"What do you mean? Speak clearly!"

Nadine tugged on Jack's sleeve. The wall was destroyed; soon there would be Magical Creatures roaming everywhere in the streets, and it would be impossible to get home. In fact, it might have been too late already.

But Jack just shook his head and leaned closer to the window. This, he knew, was essential evidence. And when one is eavesdropping on a villain, one cannot just leave before they reveal their master plan.

"Do I smell plum pudding? Sweet, sticky, overripe, rotting plum pudding?"

Frank the ogre jumped up and down and waved his arms even faster.

"That's impossible, you great oaf. That would mean that—" Crusty cut off with a snap, and Jack saw his head swivel left and right in his low armchair. He felt his stomach twist and suddenly wished he had listened to Nadine.

"Well, well," Crusty said, raising his voice. "Visitors, hmm? Come out, come out, wherever you are! Sweet little Nadine, I am so delighted to meet you."

Nadine let out an involuntary yip of fear.

Behind them, across the great expanse of the reserve, the Magical Creatures began to roar.

CHAPTER 11

It was time to flee, and flee they did.

Nadine and Jack dashed, they darted, they dove down the hill, running and tumbling and crashing through the grass, letting gravity do most of the work as they gulped in great gasps of air. There was no time for talk, no time even to look over their shoulders to see if Frank the ogre was tumbling behind them, his blue lips peeled back in a wide grin as his teeth reached for their necks with a *chomp, chomp, chomp.*

Oh, but there were dangers enough to see! Trolls hobbling toward the open gates, holding the bones of victims or the hands of grubby little troll children. Giants as tall as trees stomping across the hills with wild manes of hair that flowed down their backs. Goblins in too-small suits carrying briefcases and pickaxes, their favorite weapons. Ogres in black hats to cover their sensitive gray heads.

In short, it was a nightmare, but one the children were not going to wake up from.

They were bruised and cut and battered by the time they slowed enough to regain their footing. Nadine had crashed into a baby troll on the way and received a whack with a bone in response. Jack had barreled into a confused-looking imp who had tried to bite Jack's arm and managed only a mouthful of his borrowed jacket. Staying close together, Jack and Nadine limped on, shivering.

"I don't think they followed," Nadine said, looking back up the hill toward the house, barely visible now at such a distance. "My dad is never going to let me go out again after this."

Jack wanted to point out that no child would be allowed to go out after this, but time was short, and instead he grabbed Nadine's hand (they were practically siblings, anyway) and pulled her toward the nearest opening in the crumbling remains of the wall. They slipped through and then darted across the street, carefully avoiding an ogre family, and ran up the driveway of the nearest house.

"We can't hide forever," Nadine whispered, struggling to keep up with Jack. "They'll come here first! Looking for food!"

Jack had thought the same thing, but he tried to sound brave as he said, "We just need a good hiding spot. Until Magical Creature Control comes."

They darted among the shadows.

CHAPTER 12

"We have to split up," Nadine whispered, when they had wedged themselves into the back of a narrow shed in the side yard. Jack batted away a garden hoe that was trying to attack him. "The ogre can *smell* me."

"The ogre can smell anyone."

"Yes, but...but my smell..."

"What, plum pudding?" Jack took a sniff, but he couldn't detect it. Just a lot of rust from the shed and maybe a fruity shampoo.

"It's because of my family," Nadine whispered. All around them outside, they could hear shouts and yelps and howls. Magical Creature Control would arrive any moment to round up the creatures and lock them up until the wall could be put right.

"Everybody has something," Jack said, quoting his mother. *I do, too,* he thought.

"Yes, but—but mine is Secret."

He looked at Nadine, wondering, could it be possible? More than once he had asked his mother if there were others like him, brothers and sisters of Death. "Don't be ridiculous," she would sniff. "Death is very busy."

"Is that why they're looking for you?" Jack asked. Outside, they heard an ogre howl and launch himself at the door of the house. Inside the shed, the two children shuddered.

"I think so," Nadine whispered. "My father says it puts me in danger. It's why I have to be so careful."

"Elf blood? Mermaid blood?" Jack guessed. His ears were tingling; he wanted to ask about Death, but he was afraid of the answer.

Nadine shook her head. "I can't tell you."

"Is it from your mother's side?"

"It *is* my mother."

Jack frowned. "I'll tell you who my father is if you tell me who your mother is." Did Death have a sister? Surely not; so Nadine's Secret had to be different from his own. He had never told anyone his Secret before, but if Nadine had been able to keep hers for so long, he figured it was safe with her.

"I can't."

"But—"

The shed shook, and the door was ripped open.

"Oh, my!" said the figure before them. "Well! In all my days—oh, my!"

Nadine and Jack clutched each other, huddling in the back of the shed. Their throats were hoarse from the scream they had just released, and Jack wielded a pair of garden shears in his hand.

"Who are you?" Jack demanded.

"Who. Am. *I?*" asked the short, round little man, leaning forward to peer at them. He had a pair of goggles snug across his forehead, and was wearing a tan uniform complete with a pair of heavy black boots. "I think the more appropriate question is Who. Are. *You?* This is my shed, after all."

The heavy stomp of footsteps vibrated behind him, and the man cast a nervous glance over his shoulder. "You can go on hiding here if you wish," he said, "but you will probably not survive the night. Will you hand me those keys? No, no, the one with the kitten keychain. Thank *you.*"

Nadine handed over the keychain, which was hanging on a hook in the shed as Jack held the garden shears higher, trying to look braver than he felt. "Why did you say we wouldn't survive the night?"

"Hmm? Oh, perhaps you don't know. All the creatures have escaped from the reserve." The round man paused, waiting for some reaction, it seemed. "I expect there will be a great hullabaloo about it tomorrow. Perhaps the Army will come."

"But can't Magical Creature Control—" Nadine began.

"What, those eggheads? They can't tell a Peruvian mountain troll from a Himalayan yeti." The man laughed at his own joke, his shoulders shaking as his chest gave a few great honks. Wiping his eyes, he suddenly grew serious again. "No. No, in fact, we are all doomed. I'm Professor Blunderbunn, by the way."

"There's no university around here," Jack said.

"It is called *Online. Education,*" said Professor Blunderbunn. "And it is just as good!" He cleared his throat. "Now, if you will excuse me, I have no plans to die tonight."

"Wait!" Jack said, finally abandoning the garden shears. "Where are you going?"

"Why, to my escape vehicle."

"Can we come?" Nadine asked shyly, remembering how her father always warned her never to get in a car with a stranger.

"I should think not. There's only one seat."

"A one-seated car?" Jack said.

"A car! Pfft! What good would a car do me now? Of course not a *car*. A plane. A getaway plane." He turned on his heel to go. "If my house is still standing in the morning, would you be so kind as to check the oven? I can't remember if I left it on after baking cookies."

"Are you ever coming back?"

"Oh, certainly. But I think I'll have a hop around the world first. I can work from anywhere, you know." He gave Jack a pointed look before leaving the shed.

Nadine was trying very hard not to be frightened, which, if you have ever hidden in a shed during a Magical Creature escape, you will know is very hard to do. She was going over all of the rules her father had taught her about what to do in an emergency. Except that in her current situation she could not call the police, or Magical Creature Control, or her father. She was out of options.

"Come on," Jack said, taking her by the hand and pulling her toward the door of the shed.

"We can't go out there!" Nadine said. "The creatures—"

"We won't be out there long." He grinned, though his face looked pale. "We're catching a ride."

CHAPTER 13

Professor Blunderbunn did a quick check as he prepared to take off. Little Mittens, his naughty kitten, check. Plateful of oatmeal chocolate chip cookies wrapped in aluminum foil, check. Overnight bag, containing credit cards and his laptop, check.

"Well, Mittens," Professor Blunderbunn said, sighing. "I suppose we'd better go before those infernal creatures arrive."

Mittens mewed and sniffed questioningly at the cookie plate.

Professor Blunderbunn began to fiddle with the controls of the plane. He had bought it from the man who owned the house before him and who had impressed upon him the need to have an escape vehicle, should the wall to the reserve ever be breached. At the time, Professor Blunderbunn had been fairly sure he was being taken, but he had haggled the man down to a reasonable price, and after all, if he was ever in such grave danger, why not have a plane at the ready?

"I just wish I had bothered to practice, even once," Professor Blunderbunn muttered. Mittens looked up sharply, her tail flicking.

It really was too bad about the children, but then, it was their parents' responsibility to look after them. And what was he supposed to do, offer them the plane? They would know even less about flying it than he did.

"I'll check on them tomorrow," he told Mittens, who didn't seem to care one way or the other. His kitten was, in general, very open-minded. "The shed should hold up for a night at least. I'll drop by again in the morning before my world tour."

The engine revved up, and Professor Blunderbunn began to hum some of his favorite tunes. There really was something quite relaxing about flying, especially as the noise of the plane drowned out the sounds of shattering glass and broken dishes coming from inside his house.

"I really should not have picked a spot so close to the reserve," he said, but Mittens could not hear him over the noise of the engine. The plane began to roll forward.

The professor bumped along onto the road, which he planned to use as a narrow runway before it turned sharply off to the left. One chance, he thought, and pulled his goggles down over his eyes. The plane was very old and very rickety and made a few noises that Professor Blunderbunn was fairly sure it should not have made. But the professor only hummed louder and flipped a few switches.

"Almost, Mittens," he said, as the plane gained speed. *Bump, bump, bump* went the wheels. The curve loomed up ahead of him. Professor Blunderbunn leaned forward. He only had one shot at this, and he quite preferred not to die that night. He hadn't even had time to try the oatmeal chocolate chip cookies.

"Huzzah!" he cried, as he jerked the throttle upwards. He thought he heard a squeal and wondered briefly if it was his own or Mittens' as the plane turned sharply up and climbed into the dark sky, only narrowly cresting the line of trees. He flipped a few more switches, heard a few unpleasant pops, and soon managed to turn the plane north, in the direction of the sea.

"Well, well," he cried, the cold night air whipping about his face. He imagined the stars were close enough to touch, though in reality he was really not very much nearer to them. "What do you think of that, Mittens? FREEDOM!!"

Another squeal. Professor Blunderbunn looked left, and nearly had a heart attack. He looked right, and nearly had a stroke. Two children were riding on his wings!

"But that's..." he sputtered, wind tugging at his ears and nose. "That's just..."

The girl had sensibly wrapped her arms around the handle on one of the wings, while the boy was slipping and sliding. "Unacceptable!" cried Professor Blunderbunn. "F! F for you! No credit!"

He banged on the glass, almost forgetting to steer in the process. Finally the boy looked up, and Professor Blunderbunn motioned to the handle. Looking green, the boy crawled over and grabbed hold.

"Children!" he muttered to himself. In all of the excitement, the cookies had spilled off his lap, and two of them had fallen on the floor. "Children! Foolish children!"

Mittens looked out the window and mewed.

Somewhere around halfway through the flight, Jack realized that Professor Blunderbunn had no idea how to fly a plane.

At first he thought the jerks and zags of the plane were due merely to turbulence, which had been fun enough when he was buckled in tightly next to his mother, flying to his aunt's or his uncle's for vacation. Not so now, when every dip sent him tumbling sideways or forwards, always in danger of losing his grip.

It is not very much fun, you see, riding on the wing of a plane. I should know, having once attempted it before realizing it was much more sensible to wait on the ground.

Jack grew nervous as the professor dipped lower, presumably intending to land. Landing, Jack's cousin had once told him, was the most dangerous part of flying. He wasn't sure if it was true, but given the way Professor Blunderbunn was steering, it seemed likely.

Professor Blunderbunn mouthed something at Jack, who gripped the handle tighter. He wished he could see Nadine, check if she was alright. The ground was coming up very quickly now.

Boom! Crash! Screech!

They landed.

"What in the name of gingersnaps were you doing?" Professor Blunderbunn cried, when he had jumped out of the cockpit and onto the ground, where Nadine and Jack had already sunk. "You could have been killed!"

"We could have been killed in the shed," Nadine pointed out, her voice weak. Her hair was a complete mess, tangled all around her shoulders.

"Yes, well, at least that would have been sensible!" said the professor.

Jack looked down at his arms and his legs, quite pleasantly surprised to find that they were intact. Nadine's lips were blue, but otherwise she, too, had fared extraordinarily well for an impromptu trip on a plane's wings.

"Well, off you go, then!" said Professor Blunderbunn, shooing the children away. "Go find an adult or something."

"You're an adult," Jack said.

Professor Blunderbunn blushed. "Yes, well, I have my hands full with Mittens. But I— ah— I wish you the best of luck. On your survival." And he hopped back in his plane, tossed out the two fallen cookies, and revved the engine again. Jack and Nadine took a few steps back, huddling near the trees as Professor Blunderbunn took off in the brightening dawn.

"Where to now?" Nadine asked, looking sideways at Jack. They had been dropped off in a quiet neighborhood that Jack thought he recognized, perhaps a half-mile walk from his own home. The world seemed peaceful and quiet, as if the terrible escape of the previous night was just an unfortunate nightmare. Maybe it was.

"I suppose we should go find our parents," Jack

said, rubbing his eyes. "And take a warm bath and a nice long nap."

"My father is still on his business trip." Nadine paused. "I suppose my babysitter is worried about me."

And so the children made their next big mistake and walked back home.

CHAPTER 14

A great many cars whizzed by on their trek back. Some of them were full to the brim with suitcases and squashed bodies and dogs with heads lolling out of windows. Some were empty save for their white-faced drivers, speeding and honking their horns as if their life depended on it (I suppose, to be fair, it did). Jack and Nadine even saw one man gallop past on a horse.

"Where is everyone going?" Nadine asked, for almost all of the cars were headed in one direction, away from the town and west, where an expanse of mountains squatted.

"Away from the reserve," Jack said, his voice squeaking. Perhaps not a bad idea after all.

Once they had reached their neighborhood,

Nadine went to check in with her babysitter. Jack found he was sad to see her go, and then grew angry at himself for thinking any such thing about a girl. Booger would have laughed at him for it. Poor, gobbled-up Booger. Though maybe Booger was the lucky one after all.

"Well!" Jack's mother, Deborah, said as Jack walked in. "And just when I was ready to give up on you!"

Deborah was in a bathrobe with a shortbread cookie in one hand and a coffee mug in the other. The familiar sight of her filled Jack with joy, and he felt an almost irrepressible urge to hug her. But luckily, he just managed to suppress it. Hugs were not for boys of his age.

"Mom," Jack said, "the reserve wall—it's gone."

"Everyone knows that." Deborah reached down and planted a large kiss on Jack's cheek before he could duck it. Her bushy brown hair was sticking up in all directions, and she had so far only globbed a bit of eye shadow on. "The mayor sent an emergency warning. They've set up temporary shelter in the mountains. Mandatory evacuation."

Jack's eyes widened.

"Oh, yes. And imagine my surprise when I find my only son's gone! I think to myself, if he's gets home alive, I will throttle him myself." She shook her fists menacingly, but Deborah Hallows' most violent act had been to throw a crumbled shortbread biscuit in the trash. "Well, go on, then. Go get a clean pair of underwear and a book. We're getting out of here."

Just then, they heard a knock on the door.

"Is it a troll?" Deborah called, as she packed up cookies in a duffel bag sprawled on the breakfast table. "Don't answer it, Jack. I'm sure I have my electric zizzer somewhere in here. That self-defense class was worth *something* at least."

The doorbell rang.

"Don't answer it!" Deborah warned again, trotting up the stairs as Jack looked out the front window. "I'll be down in a minute. Pack, pack!"

But Jack, who wisely ascertained that trolls and ogres would likely not knock, had spotted Nadine standing by the front door, looking small and tired and worried in her coat and pajamas. Jack realized he was still in the same uniform—and in Nadine's coat, no less—and blushed.

"My babysitter is gone," Nadine said, in a near whisper, when Jack opened the door. "Where is everyone?"

"Mandatory evacuation," Jack said, pulling her inside. Deborah thundered back down the stairs.

"What did I—?! Oh, Nadine, dear, how are you? How is your father?"

"On a business trip, Mrs. Hallows."

"When is he not? Do you need a lift to the mountains?"

Nadine looked at Jack, confused. He nodded for her. "Can she ride with us, Mom?"

"Of course. Are you packed yet? Nadine, I do hope you brought some spare underwear."

Twenty minutes later, the two Hallows and the young Jang were packed into the old station wagon, a much more pleasant mode of transport than the wings of a rickety plane. Like Professor Blunderbunn, Deborah had the good sense to bring a plate of cookies with her, though I'm sorry to say they were only of the shortbread variety.

"Posh!" she said irritably, as they pulled onto the main road. It was almost deserted; they were one of the last few out of the neighborhood. "Put on some country music, would you, Jack? I do hate jazz."

"That's classical music," Nadine said from the backseat. She had not had time to go back for any clothes, and so had a backpack full of Deborah's "skinny clothes," most of which Nadine planned to avoid with all her power.

"It's jazz. Can't you hear the saxophone?" Deborah said, jerking left to change lanes as a violin played over the radio. Jack switched the station. "Now, Jack, are you going to tell me what you were up to last night?"

Jack looked sideways at his mother, who was still dressed in her bathrobe, though she had pulled on a pair of athletic shorts and a T-shirt beneath it. She was a tax accountant, a job that to Jack seemed unable to contain the wide expanse of his mother's personality: quirky, placid, scatterbrained, but occasionally capable of a laser focus that could tear apart any problem.

"Does it have to do with Booger?" Deborah asked. Jack nodded. "Did you go to the reserve? Did you tear down the wall?"

"What? No!" cried Jack, and Nadine stifled a giggle. His mother seemed inexplicably relieved by this—why would she even suspect it? "We went there—"

"We?"

"Nadine and me."

"Ah. I see." Deborah arched one eyebrow as she looked at Nadine in the rear-view mirror. Nadine pretended to look out the window.

"A man did it. Crusty, I think. He called someone, and he gave an order, and his ogre brother ate another man—"

"Slow down, Jack. One detail at a time."

He took a great breath, and together with Nadine,

managed to tell his mother most of what had happened that night. They left out the impromptu flight with Professor Blunderbunn, instead telling her they ran back home.

"Hmm," Deborah said, when they had finished. In the back, Nadine watched in awe. At this point, her father would almost certainly have fainted with worry, or gone green and then red and then erupted in a whole slew of colorful language about the Importance of Safety and Nadine's Utter Disregard For Her Own Well-Being.

But Deborah seemed quite calm, her fingers drumming on the steering wheel as she took the turn-off to the mountains, where they joined a long line of traffic.

"Well," Deborah finally said, "I do think we are in quite a pickle here."

CHAPTER 15

There are not many towns that are unfortunate enough to be situated quite so near to a reserve. In fact, I would bet that you had never before heard of one. The towns, after all, do not advertise the fact. It often ruins the tourism (or attracts exactly the wrong kind of tourist).

But Jack's town was one of them, and it had prepared for the worst by creating a mountain evacuation zone, built precisely for this sort of doomsday scenario. The idea was that the townspeople could race up there in the event of a mass escape and hunker down while Magical Creature Control sorted everything out.

Unfortunately, the villains also knew all this and had prepared accordingly.

So while the station wagon containing Jack,

Nadine, and Deborah puttered up the hill, playing country music and filling up with the scent of buttery shortbreads, and while trolls and ogres and every kind of nasty creature you could imagine wandered the streets of the town below, the masterminds of the evil plot hunkered down in a windowless, cramped room to put the rest of their plan into action.

"Nadine," they said, the words growling and sputtering as they left their evil throats. "Get Nadine."

A small man, often overlooked in such meetings, cleared his throat. "And Jack Hallows," he spat out. "We need Jack Hallows, too."

"Take a number!" the pale, puffy-faced woman shrieked as the townsfolk streamed inside the compound. "Take a number! Stay in line! *For the love of all things beautiful, STAY IN LINE!*"

Most people obeyed, loudly complaining about the cramped quarters, eyeing with dislike the cots set up all across the wide space of the gymnasium. "Yes, but aren't there some private quarters?" the richer folks would ask, trying to press a crisp bill into the puffy-faced woman's hand. They were all handed the same survival pack in response—filled with a toothbrush and a generic brand of deodorant—and told they were allowed one cot per person.

"Will my father know to come here?" asked Nadine anxiously, as they moved up in line. Deborah offered the children some shortbread and began popping the biscuits in her mouth.

"I'm sure he'll be telephoned," said Deborah vaguely. "Oh, lovely! Do these come in pink?"

The man handing out blankets gave Deborah a confused look and moved on.

The great gymnasium was soon vibrating with the shouts and cries and arguments of the townsfolk, along with the barks of all the dogs brought along for the evacuation. Deborah, Nadine, and Jack picked three cots near the back, after which Deborah told the children to stay put and she would find some food.

"Your mother is wonderful," Nadine whispered when Deborah had left. "Is she always like that?"

"I suppose so," said Jack, not understanding. "Though she doesn't usually wear her bathrobe out."

"Well, well," said a familiar and most unwelcome voice. "Would you look at this?"

The next thing Jack felt was a punch to his stomach.

Urkel Underbottom had been smarter this time. He had brought back up.

His most trusted goon, Stringy, held back Jack's

arms as Urkel delivered yet another punch to Jack's gut.

Wait! you say. *Where were all the adults? Why wasn't anybody stopping to help?*

Well, you see, the adults were all dealing with their own problems—namely, the fact that they had just been evacuated after the most frightening news of their lives. They had more important things to worry about, such as locating all of their families and making sure they secured the non-lumpy pillows to sleep on.

And besides, adults are very good at missing anything that they do not want to see. It is one of their fatal flaws.

Two more of Urkel's goons hung back, mostly to cheer the revolting bully on as he pummeled Jack yet again.

"Stop!" Nadine cried. "You're hurting him!"

This resulted in a chorus of laughter, Urkel bending over his knees and taking in great gasps of air as he let out a low chortle. Stringy allowed himself a small giggle, still holding Jack's arms tight. Jack, for his part, blushed red, managing to feel a good deal of embarrassment through his pain.

"Little Jackie has a girlfriend!" Urkel taunted, when he had recovered his breath. He delivered another punch, and Jack's whole body vibrated with the blow. He struggled against Stringy's sweaty palms, fighting to hold back the tears that were coming to his eyes.

Suddenly, Urkel let out a high-pitched yip that drew a few eyes their way. The great bully looked down at the fist he had just been pulling back for another punch, his lower lip trembling as he saw the thin scratches Nadine had left on his skin.

For a moment, all were still. The bullies' desire for revenge battling with their puny senses of honor, which told them, in their mothers' shrill voices, that they should never hit a girl.

Urkel leapt for Nadine.

"Hey!" Jack shouted, struggling against Stringy, whose mouth was gaping open like a fish. He managed to elbow the greasy fellow in the solar plexus, which is quite a good spot to strike a bully, if you must know.

Urkel had grabbed hold of Nadine's hair, yanking her backwards as he pulled back his other arm for a punch (Urkel's repertoire of violence was, at that time, severely limited). Urkel's two other goons had fled. Stringy was doubled over gasping.

Jack knocked into Urkel like a battering ram. It felt like slamming into a stone wall. Urkel did not move, only gave a little snort of surprise and loosened his grip on Nadine. The three were soon interlocked in a tornado of scratches and punches and hair-pulling.

Jack felt an elbow in his chest, and then fingernails on his back, and then a foot stomping his toes. He tried to focus on Urkel's yowling face, winding his own arm back for one good punch—

"What is the meaning of this?"

The children sprang apart, gasping. Stringy took the opportunity to disappear into the crowd.

Ubork Underbottom stood before them, his arms crossed over his broad chest, his craggy face scowling down at them. "Urkel!" he demanded. "What is the meaning of this?"

"He just came over and starting hitting Jack," Nadine accused. Her hair was wild, and she had a bruise across one of her cheeks. Jack felt another surge of embarrassment at having a girl defend him, though he was equally impressed that quiet, rule-following Nadine had gotten into a fight for him.

Ubork acted as though he had not heard her answer, which, in fact, might have been the case. Ubork suffered from terrible earwax.

"Nothing," huffed Urkel. *"He's* the one who threw food at me yesterday."

Ubork swung his gaze back to Jack, who blushed. I know what you did, Jack thought. You helped those men unleash the Magical Creatures.

Ubork was not an enemy he wished to have at the moment.

"That was you, eh?" Ubork said, raising his voice. "Do you realize how hard it is to get tomato stains out, you nasty little child?"

"Excuse me!"

Deborah pushed her way closer, holding three steaming cups of hot chocolate balanced between her hands. Urkel sniffed hopefully, but Deborah leaned toward Nadine and Jack with her offerings.

"So you're the mother," Ubork sneered.

"What's going on?" Deborah said to Jack, ignoring Ubork.

Nadine tried to speak, but Urkel cut her off, putting on his best teacher's-pet voice (which was, to anyone with half a brain, quite unconvincing). "Jack attacked me," he whimpered, and even made his lower lip tremble. "I— I—" And he held up his hand, which in the scuffle had received the smallest of scratches, the teeniest of pricks, the itty-bittiest of cuts. One single drop of blood welled out.

Blood, you see, is a trump card.

"That savage!" cried Ubork, leaping forward as if to pummel Jack himself. Urkel snickered behind his father's back and covered it with a sob when his father turned around.

Deborah moved to intercept the elder Under-bottom. "Now, just hold on, there—"

"I'll have you thrown out! All of you! To think,

we escaped trolls and ogres only to find such vicious brutes!"

"*You* didn't escape anything," Jack said, holding his hot chocolate in trembling hands. Ubork Underbottom whipped back around to him, and Jack regretted his words. The anger there, the evil, was something he knew he should steer clear of.

"Neither. Will. You," Ubork promised.

Just then, a Reaper slipped into the gymnasium, as a portly man spoke over the loudspeaker.

"Town meeting!" his heavy voice called. "Town meeting! Gather round!"

CHAPTER 16

There is almost nothing as boring as listening to a bunch of adults talk. Think of being stuck in a room with your teacher for an hour (sometimes called *class*) and multiply that by two hundred. Then you will get some idea of how excruciating a town meeting can be.

But, alas, the adults seemed to like it, because they could hear the pleasing sound of their own voices and grow righteously angry at anyone who dared disagree with them. It is one of the few pleasures left to adults.

Nadine and Jack sat behind Deborah, sipping their hot chocolate and nursing their wounds, hoping that someone would finally stand up and say something sensible, like *We must find the people who did this and make sure they can't do anything bad ever again.*

But the adults were not doing that. They were playing a very fun (to them) game of Whose Fault Is This and Where Should My Finger Be Pointing?

The owner of the construction company responsible for building the wall was called a cheap and careless man.

The family responsible for maintaining the reserve grounds was called a pack of fiends.

The mayor, who had voted to keep the reserve in town year after year (it led to some very nice tax breaks for the residents), was called a selfish, greedy, and short-sighted politician.

But no one brought up the group of villains that Nadine and Jack had seen that night. Could it be that they were the only ones who knew? No one even bothered blaming Ubork Underbottom, who after all, was just guarding the gate, and certainly couldn't have been responsible for the sudden crumbling of the entire wall.

"Mom," Jack whispered, leaning forward to where his mother sat, watching the scene in silence. "Don't they know who destroyed the wall?"

Deborah raised her hand. "Excuse me," she boomed, "but don't any of you know who destroyed the wall?"

The townspeople all began to speak at once. It was the wind, one person said. Nonsense, it was a pack of raging ogres, said another. I heard it was Peevy Parsons, said a third. Peevy Parsons the billionaire? asked a fourth. Someone else confirmed that Peevy was building himself a private Magical Creature collection and could very well have been stealing some of theirs.

"What a load of hogwash," Deborah muttered. Jack felt a pair of eyes on him from across the room, and looked up to see Ubork Underbottom staring daggers at him. He shivered.

"They don't know," Nadine whispered anxiously. "Nobody knows about the men. About Crusty."

"They'll figure it out," said Jack, with more confidence than he felt.

"Can your mom help?"

He shook his head. Nadine had too much faith in parents. Yes, Deborah was brave, and smart, and very good with numbers, but she would be entirely helpless at defeating a conspiracy of evil villains. Really, once you were over the age of fourteen, your villain-defeating powers significantly diminished, especially if you never practiced.

"Enough of this!" shouted a woman, clutching her two boxy-looking children to her chest. She looked like a string bean, with a wisp of blonde hair tied into a ponytail atop her bony, pointed head. "When is Magical Creature Control going to round all of them up? *When can we go home?*"

The mayor, who was leading the meeting, mopped his brow and wished once again that he had just been a dentist, as his mother had wished. "Soon, soon," he muttered.

"Soon isn't good enough!"

"They're not doing anything," another man called. "My wife runs their Collections Division. She said they've only caught three so far!"

"Three? Three!" the rest of the crowd cried, incredulous.

"When are they going to catch the rest?"

"How on earth is that going to help anybody?"

"Have they patched up the wall yet?"

"Do we need to leave town for good?"

"Please, please," the mayor pleaded, rapping the podium to gain the townspeople's attention.

"We need to flee!"

"We need to fly!"

"We can't stay here—they'll kill us all!"

"They're probably marching up the hill as we speak!"

"They'll grind our bones!"

"They'll chew us up!"

"They'll smash us to bits!"

"THERE ARE CHILDREN PRESENT."

A moment of silence followed, and then the voices picked up again, louder and more chaotic than before.

"Oh, my," Deborah said. "I do think we're in quite the pickle. *Quite* the pickle."

Jack and Nadine exchanged a nervous glance. This was not how the meeting was supposed to go. This was not fixing anything.

"We need to do something," Jack whispered to Nadine. He wished Booger was there. Booger would have looked at him, wide-eyed and afraid, and Jack would feel braver because he would need to have courage for the both of them.

Nadine, though she looked frightened, had a steely edge of determination in her eyes. It made Jack feel that perhaps he was not as brave as he pretended after all. He would not have minded, really, if Booger had talked him out of interfering.

"Okay," Nadine said. "What do we do?"

The Grim Reaper crept closer to the stage, where the mayor was standing and watching the chaos all around him. The mayor very much wanted to go back home, to his wide apartment with its bay windows and plush rugs, where he could play classical music and read presidential biographies in peace. If not a dentist, why could he have not been a professor?

Or an art critic? Or a bookseller?

Too many people, the mayor thought, trying not to let the panic get the best of him. It rested like a great pressure on his chest. Too many people who needed him, whose lives were in danger all because of the crumbled wall, the wall that the mayor had insisted, year after year, would be strong enough to hold back the creatures in the reserve. How many would fall to the attacks before Magical Creature Control rounded them all up? *If* Magical Creature Control rounded them all up?

The mayor gasped for air. The Grim Reaper reached out for him. The pressure in the mayor's chest grew.

He fell to the floor as the Reaper made off with his soul. It was a full minute, I am sad to say, before anyone even noticed. The mayor's poor heart had given out.

Did you think it would be another troll attack? There are other ways that people die, you know.

CHAPTER 17

If you believe that the worst thing that happened in the mountain evacuation zone was a dead mayor, then perhaps you should stop reading here. Because when Magical Creatures escape their reserve, a great many terrible things take place, and a town cannot just get away with a dead mayor and a few broken windows.

Still hopeful, are you? Well, so was everyone else in town, even as two brave volunteers offered to take the mayor to the hospital (too late, I'm afraid), and as the others looked around, frightened, feeling that this first death would attract many others (not generally true, but close enough).

The town's leader was gone, and though no one had really listened to him, the town felt the void like a sock of Urkel's fist to their stomachs. Who would lead them now? Who would reassure them that everything would be alright? Who would stand up and take the blame when things went wrong?

The townspeople all looked about at one another, hoping someone would have the answer.

One person did.

It was not the person that they should have trusted, I'm afraid.

CHAPTER 18

A suit is a very useful tool in the adult world. It says to others: *look at me! I am a respectable gentleman! I probably have a job and an income! I don't wear socks with my sandals and I probably disapprove of the same things you do!*

Some suits speak differently than others, but that is the gist of it. And this man, Chester Charles, knew the value of a suit quite well.

He ascended to the stage slowly, hampered by his considerable girth. Chester had always felt that, had he not been so short, he would not have been nearly as fat, and he hated the former fact ten times more than the latter. Recently, his shape had taken such an odd turn that his suits had to be custom-made, let out around the waist and tapered grotesquely about the neck, where his squat, small, lemon-shaped head resided.

"Crusty," gasped Jack.

Nadine gaped. The two children drew closer together on instinct, even as the adults fell silent and turned to watch this unknown man ascend to the stage, lowering the microphone that the mayor had left.

"Well," he said solemnly. It was, without a doubt, Crusty the shadow man, and Nadine and Jack looked about nervously for his ogre brother. None of the other townsfolk seemed concerned.

One woman rudely squawked, "Who are you?"

"Mom," Jack said, tugging on Deborah's sleeve. "He's— last night—" But Jack's voice caught in his throat. Just a few rows down, an extraordinarily large and extraordinarily ugly lady in a summer hat turned to look back at him. She was wearing a garish amount of makeup and a rumpled long-sleeved dress that reached down to her splayed, oversized feet.

It was the ogre.

And it was smiling right at Jack.

Jack leaned back, and slowly, though the ogre's head remained cocked to the side, the horrible thing turned back around. It'll gobble us up, Jack thought, his heart thumping in his chest.

Nadine had seen the ogre, too, and shot Jack a panicked look.

"What were you saying, dear?" Deborah asked, but Crusty began speaking again, and a few rude old ladies hushed them.

"I am a government man," Crusty started, to a chorus of groans. "But not from any division you will have heard of. I am one of the Fixers."

He let this title sink into people's minds. Words have power, you see, especially when they are let loose to flutter and flap about on their own.

"Fixers are called to help in the worst situations, the worst Magical Creature catastrophes. We know every emergency protocol designed to ensure your safety. We know every evacuation route, every secret cellar, every classified defensive maneuver against these animals."

The ugly ogre grunted in its dress.

"Some of the measures that I suggest may seem drastic to you. But we Fixers are brought in as a last resort. When there is otherwise no hope of a…successful recapture." Crusty peered out at the crowd, his little head swiveling left and right. A few stray puffs of yellow-white hair only emphasized the lemonness of his head. "My question for you is, *are you ready?*"

Silence followed. The adults looked uneasily about—happy, yes, to be under someone's authority once more—but not liking this "drastic" business at all.

"What are you proposing?" one man called out.

Crusty drew his hands together and sighed. The speakers crackled with the noise. "It is of utmost importance," he said, "to start sorting the Unfortunates."

Deborah gripped the bottom of her seat, her knuckles growing white.

"Mom?" Jack asked, as murmurs rippled through the crowd. Nadine looked ill.

"No," Deborah muttered. "No…he can't…it's illegal!"

One of the old women who had hushed her previously whipped around. "It's an emergency!" she hissed. "He can do whatever he likes."

Deborah shook herself. "Where's his license?" she asked loudly. "His identification? Why should we trust him?"

"Mom," Jack said, his heart giving another lurch as the ogre looked back toward them. It licked its lip-sticked lips. "Mom!"

But no one was paying Deborah Hallows any mind. They were thinking of their abandoned homes, their poor little children, their comforting routines. If this man could save all of those, why, then he was certainly to be trusted. Someone else asked Crusty (respectfully calling him Mr. Charles) just how, exactly, they would need to be sorted.

Again, Crusty brought his hands together and

sighed. The speakers crackled. "We need to find everyone with the Golden Bloodlines," he said. "And separate them immediately."

"But why?"

"Right now?"

"Separate them how?"

"Silence, please!" Crusty called. "Some of my associates will help you. We have experimental kits if you are not sure of your particular bloodline. If you have any lineage of elf or mermaid or fairy or what have you, we will bus you immediately to a separate evacuation zone. Golden Bloodlines must be separated from the Black right away."

Jack felt a prickle of sweat on his forehead. He was Black, along with anyone with troll or ogre or gnome or goblin blood. His mother, she had told him once, was as free from bloodlines as it was possible to be, though she did have a great aunt who was half-Red Dwarf (the creature, not the star).

"Humans will stay with the Black Bloodlines," Crusty continued, as the buzz in the crowd grew louder. "Our first priority is separating the Goldens."

"But why?" a few of the men and women wailed. Husbands and wives clutched hands; friends looked nervously about, as if trying to remember which of them belonged to which camp.

"The Golden Bloodlines are most vulnerable,"

said Crusty, rubbing the side of his pale face with one hand. "The creatures will go after them first. We must insure their safety."

"Jack," Nadine whispered. She was pale as a ghost. *"Jack."*

He glanced over at her.

"What is he going to do?"

Jack looked down at the ogre, who was moving silently toward the stage. He shivered. "What are you?"

Nadine bit her lip, and shook her head.

"Golden or Black?" Jack said impatiently. As if her Secret was any worse than his!

"Golden," Nadine whispered.

"You'll just have to go. Let him take you somewhere safe with the others." Indeed, the protests of the crowd were mostly dying down, and the Golden Bloodlines were moving off to one side. To Jack they looked strong and kind and imperious, the type of people he wished to stay with. The Black Bloodlines, on the other hand, looked surly and suspicious and mean. He wondered that he had never noticed the differences before. And then he saw Urkel, snarling at a few Golden Bloods that passed.

"I can't leave you with him!" Nadine said, glancing back up at Crusty. "Or his…his brother."

Deborah turned back toward them. Her eyes were flashing. "I don't like this. I don't like this one bit."

"Mrs. Hallows—"

"Which are you, my dear? Golden? Well, in that case, you might as well get out of here. Something's not right, and you won't want to be around when we find out what that is." She sighed and ran one hand through Jack's hair. Normally he would have recoiled at the public affection, but now he just wished his mother could somehow make all their problems go away. "If only you could pass as one, darling. But you're Black, through and through."

Indeed, a few lines had formed for the experimental kits that Crusty had mentioned. Frowning workers in suits stood with black suitcases, within which were glowing green squares with two spiked teeth on each end. These would be pressed over each subject's hand, and the squares would buck and squeeze, the tiny teeth drawing blood.

"Black!" they would squawk.

Or, "Gold!"

Or, "Cap-oo-ey!" Jack assumed that this meant there was no lineage to speak of.

"I want to stay with you," Nadine said quickly.

"We'll be alright," Deborah said, but Jack saw the worry in her eyes. "You go with the others, dear. We'll see you soon enough."

"But—"

"Last call!" one of the suited men shouted.

"Already?" Nadine cried. Deborah gave her a friendly little push in the direction of the Golden Bloods. One of them, a tall woman with bright blue eyes, wrapped one arm around Nadine's shoulder and tried to calm her. But Nadine only shook her head, looking back tearfully at Jack and Deborah before she was herded out the doors and onto a waiting bus.

CHAPTER 19

"Mom," Jack said urgently. "I have to tell you something."

The ogre was gone, and Crusty had disappeared from sight. Jack needed to explain to his mother how much danger they were all in, how Crusty probably had something terrible planned for those left behind.

"Jack," Deborah said, sighing as she turned around. They were one of the few people left in their seats; most were swarming around, shouting about how *they* should be on the bus, that yes, they might have three generations of troll blood in them, but there was also a fairy in there somewhere.

"We can't stay here. It's not safe. Nadine—"

"Jack, hush," Deborah said, shaking her head. "It's not safe anywhere. Not anymore."

"But that man—!"

"I need to tell you something," Deborah said, in the tone of voice she used when Jack knew he had better be quiet and listen.

"Okay," Jack said, though he couldn't stop fidgeting.

"I know who Nadine is," Deborah said, rubbing her eyes. Eye shadow smeared over her brow. "You have to be careful, Jack. You have to be very, very careful."

"What do you mean?"

"She seems like a lovely young girl. But there's a reason her father keeps her under such tight rein." She paused. "I might take a page out of his book, really."

Jack shook his head, not understanding.

"Her mother," Deborah said, hesitating. "It's not my place to tell you. But I am not sure the two of you should be spending time together. I know after Booger—"

"But she's a Golden Blood, Mom! And I'm—"

"Hush! I know exactly what you are. There, enough of that. I've told you once, and we won't speak of it again." Her breath grew quick and short, as it did whenever Jack asked too many questions.

But never mind that, Jack thought. He wasn't going to waste time arguing about Nadine when there were more pressing problems at hand. Namely, the very great danger they were already in.

"Mom," Jack started, but just then, the room exploded.

Alright, *exploded* is perhaps a bit hyperbolic. But if you were there, that is exactly what you would have thought at first.

The doors to the gymnasium burst open, and dozens of men in black boots and military uniforms strode in. They all had horrible haircuts and wore dark sunglasses.

"Oh, my," Deborah said. "Jack, stay close."

Jack did, but he had a very strange sensation: up until that point in his life, it was his mother who had most often looked after him. But now, as he was growing bigger, and older, and stronger, he had the strong sense that it was his turn to look after her.

"It's okay," Jack said, as his mother squeezed his hand. She looked at him, her face unreadable, as they fell back.

"Gather round!" called Crusty, reappearing. He looked even fatter and shorter standing next to the uniformed men. A space had been cleared near the cots, and Jack briefly wondered whether all of the Golden Bloods had had time to collect their things.

"We're going to sort all of you by creature!"

"It's not fair!" cried one man. "We deserve to be

safe, too!"

A crooked smile came over Crusty's face.

"Where did you take my husband?" asked one woman, leaning on the shoulder of another woman with the same slim build and dark, curly hair. "It's not fair! You can't split us up like this!"

"Do you mean to say," said Crusty solemnly, "that your husband left you behind? To go with the other Golden Bloods?"

The woman's cheeks turned red and she buried her face in her companion's shoulder.

"Listen up, please!" called Crusty, spinning around so that his voice carried to all corners of the room. The Black Bloods (and other ragtag people left behind) inched nearer, huddled in their small family units. "I had to remove the Golden Bloods—all of the Golden Bloods—for one very strong reason."

He paused for effect. Jack glanced at his mother, who was chewing nervously on her lower lip. She had somehow procured another shortbread, and bit into it, spilling crumbs down her front. When she saw Jack looking at her, she winked, but there was no laughter in her face.

"The Golden Bloods are responsible for the release of the Magical Creatures."

Gasps went through the crowd. The Black Bloods looked around, incredulous, even as Jack's mouth gaped open.

"Why, that's just—"

"Impossible!"

"Could it be?"

"I thought they were up to something!"

"Mom," Jack said urgently, "that can't be true. Last night—"

"Jack."

His mother's voice sliced through his protests, through the cries and protestations of the crowd. He had never seen her look so deadly serious, her face set, her eyes flashing, her lips trembling as she wiped the last few crumbs from them.

She turned and kneeled down next to Jack.

"Listen to me," she said urgently, "I need you to do something. Jack? Jack, pay attention." He had been looking back at Crusty, who was now giving some sort of speech on the conspiracy of the Golden Bloods to rid the world of the Black Creatures and anyone who shared their blood.

"Namely, all of you," Crusty said seriously, to another chorus of gasps.

"Jack!" Jack turned back to his mother. "Are you listening?"

Jack nodded.

"I'm going to have to go away for a few hours. And leave you alone. I need you to stay here, okay?

Whatever happens, do not leave. You have to stay with everyone else, alright?"

Jack's mouth was dry. He struggled to find his words. "Why?"

Deborah kissed him on the forehead, wet and prickly. "Just promise me you'll listen. I love you."

"I love you, too. But—"

"Stay, Jack. I don't ask much of you." Her gaze flitted between his two eyes, trying to read his intentions there. Jack remained frozen, unable to reconcile his mother's sudden attitude and the treacherous lies of Crusty. Did she know? Did she understand? Why did she look so afraid?

"I'll come back soon," she promised, and she turned away quickly before Jack could determine whether that faint glimmer in her eye was indeed a tear.

And then she left him alone.

CHAPTER 20

"So you see," Crusty finished, "we had to remove anyone involved in the conspiracy immediately from the vicinity, before they could finish their evil plot."

"My husband wouldn't plot against me," the same slim, dark-haired woman said.

"Are you sure?"

The woman's mouth gaped like a fish. A sea of faces turned toward her—angry, suspicious, accusing faces. She *was* sure, but could she say that to them?

"Unless," Crusty suggested, "you are on his side...?"

"N-n-no!" said the woman, recoiling. "No. I'm a Black Blood. A Black Blood!" She erupted in another fit of sobs, confused and frightened, and the rest of the crowd who had Golden Blood family resolved then and there to remain silent about it.

"Well," said another man, short and knobby, with a chin twice as large as his forehead. "What do we do, then?"

"Simple," Crusty explained, relishing their attention, savoring the smoothness with which his master plot was coming off. First this town, then the world.

They would need to preempt any attack by the Golden Bloods. Crusty and his men had taken care of that for now, by carting off the Golden Bloods in government buses, provided by the Fixers. The next stage would be ensuring that the Golden Bloods could never attack again.

"It is time we allied ourselves with the right kind," Crusty said, and it was then that the ogre—still dressed in its unfashionable gown and summer hat—stepped up next to him.

It took the adults a few minutes to understand just exactly what Crusty was suggesting. They were sidetracked for a time by their fear of the ogre.

"What a vile, disgusting, ugly beast!" cried an old woman, clutching her rubbery arms to her body. She was, in fact, descended from three generations of ogre-tainted blood.

"Save the children!" shouted another, and for thirty seconds all of the children, Jack included, were violently pushed toward the back. Jack found himself just a few feet away from Urkel, who mimed strangling Jack before another boy fell into him, knocking Urkel sideways.

"Peace, peace!" cried Crusty. Jack was pinned against the back wall, a few smaller (and, truth be told, a few older) children crying around him. "The ogre will bring you no harm. I'm sorry to say that you have been lied to for quite some time. The real enemies are not the ogres and trolls and goblins—how could they be, when they are your ancestors?"

"From very far back," huffed one woman.

"Perhaps so, perhaps so. But they are not your enemies. The Golden Bloods are." He paused, waiting for this latest information to sink in. Lies, you see, have to be layered upon one another, coaxed and stretched and patted down. And Crusty was very experienced at selling them.

Jack wanted to shout out, *It's not true!* He didn't think Crusty had gotten a good look at him the night before, but he would love to see the evil man's expression when he revealed just what he knew. But too many people were talking, and more and more children squeezed toward the back, away from the gaping smile of the ogre. Jack was pushed into a corner, unable to move, let alone speak.

And besides, if he said something, he'd give up his one chance to put his plan into action.

Because Jack was not going to sit around—whatever his mother said—and let Crusty do something to the Golden Bloods. Not when good, loyal Booger would have been one of them, not when his new friend Nadine was there, too.

The urgency of his mission was confirmed only a minute later, when Crusty's face broke into a nasty smile.

"We will kill the traitorous leaders of the Golden Bloods," he said, tugging on the lapels of his expensive suit. "And trap the rest in the Magical Creature reserve. Our brethren will roam free."

CHAPTER 21

The men in sunglasses began their work, sorting the remaining townspeople into their bloodlines. Jack slipped away, looking around once more for any sign of his mother. But she was gone, and despite her request, Jack would soon be, too.

He, after all, had never officially promised.

Jack was just about to reach the back door when he heard heavy breathing in the shadows. He froze, looking at a hulking outline lurking in the corner.

Jack made a few more footstep noises by pumping his legs up and down in place.

"Gotcha!" Urkel shouted, swinging his arms at where Jack would have been had he actually walked anywhere. Urkel's hands closed over empty air, and he gave a little cry of disappointment as he went tumbling, his goon Stringy tripping behind him.

"Morning, Urkel," said Jack amiably. "Practicing your troll moves?"

"I don't need to practice those!" Urkel spat, his face tomato red. Stringy scrambled back up, wiping dust off the front of his shirt as he laughed, a beat too late, at Urkel's response.

Jack glanced toward the door behind Urkel. It was his best bet; the others were alarmed, save for the guarded front door. He could try darting around Urkel, but it would be all too easy for one of the two bullies to reach out and snatch him. And Jack didn't like his odds, trapped in the dark corner of the gymnasium with two fiendish boys, the adults too preoccupied to pay them much attention.

"Where are you going, Jackie?" said Urkel. "You a Golden Blood? Did you miss your bus?"

Oh, how I'd like to tell him, thought Jack, heat creeping to his face. Urkel liked to go and on about how many creatures he had in his family, how his great-great-grandfather was some sort of troll king (though who knew what that meant), and how this gave him all sorts of special powers and privileges over everyone else.

But Jack knew how to keep a Secret.

"Just an early morning stroll. You know they're serving cake for lunch?"

Urkel snorted, though Stringy looked up hopefully. Urkel enjoyed violence more than sweets, which made him an almost invincible bully. "The only thing I want for lunch is a Jack sandwich."

Stringy tittered.

Jack weighed his options. Turn around and wait for his mother to sort things out (she was, after all, very good at it), or make a run for the door and put his plan into action.

Right. As if giving up were a real choice.

Urkel was ready for him. Jack darted forward, but Urkel dove sideways, smashing into Jack as he reached for the door.

"Grab his ankles!" Urkel called, and Stringy made a clumsy swipe for Jack's legs as Jack scrambled up, pushing on the bar of the door while Urkel wrapped him in a (very ill-intentioned) bear hug.

Jack struggled as Urkel pummeled him, hitting him again and again in the stomach and chest. He gasped for breath, trying to wriggle his way out of Urkel's death grip. Stringy delivered a few kicks for good measure until Urkel snapped that he was spoiling his fun.

Bruised and exhausted, his lip bleeding, Jack scrambled once more for the door. He was only inches away when Urkel grabbed him, laughing. He pushed Jack to the ground again, letting Jack struggle for the handle of the door, just out of reach. Stringy and Urkel guffawed as he reached helplessly for it.

"You're not going anywhere," Urkel said. "Your girlfriend's gonna get it, just like Booger."

Jack had been flailing in Urkel's iron grip, already knowing he was too small and too weak to break free. But the mention of Booger did something to him. He felt a surge of strength, as if Booger was there watching him, rooting for him.

Jack spun around, fist curled, and socked Urkel right in the face.

The howl must have drawn some attention. That was Jack's last thought before he jumped through the door and made it outside.

There wasn't time to worry, though. There was hardly any time at all.

Now, up until that point, Jack's main offenses had been limited to disrupting class, throwing lasagna, and talking back to rude bullies. The most that will get you is detention, and maybe a little extra attention from bullies such as Urkel. But now Jack had to think on a grander scale.

First up, stealing a car.

Jack didn't know how to drive, of course, but he couldn't worry about the details. Instead, he sprinted over to the nearest car, trying the front door and letting out a grunt of frustration when he found it locked. He tried this twice more before a door finally opened, and he leapt inside just as Urkel pushed his way out the back door, followed by Ubork Underbottom, Crusty, and the ogre.

Hurry hurry hurry, Jack chanted to himself. He leaned over to the glove box, snapping it open. Once, while sitting in the front seat of his mother's car, Jack had popped open the glove box and found a spare key. "Heavens, how long has that been in there?" his mother had cried, taking it and pocketing it. She had plum forgotten about it after the purchase of the car.

It was a long shot, but there wasn't time to come up with a better plan. Jack shoved aside the papers and napkins, and his hand closed over a key. A surge of adrenaline shot through him.

He remembered to lock the doors just as Urkel smacked into the driver's side. The ogre lumbered toward him, close behind, and with shaking hands Jack pushed the key into the ignition, and turned it just as he had seen his mother do so many times.

"Yes!" Jack cried, when he heard the rev of an engine. But then there was the whole matter of actually driving the car.

Ubork Underbottom was shouting something at him, positioning himself in front of the vehicle's grille and slapping his hands against the hood. On Jack's left, Urkel continued to try the door, shouting curses that Jack blissfully could not hear.

The ogre lumbered up, reached down, and lifted the front end of the car.

Jack let out a small yip as he moved the handle next to him to "reverse," the car tilting a couple inches. He yanked on his seatbelt as he pressed the gas, and the car jerked and reared back, the ogre losing his grip. The figure of Ubork retreated in the distance, and a cloud of dust rose and obscured Jack's view.

He switched to drive, and jolted forward.

CHAPTER 22

"WAHOOO!" cried Jack, for even though he was being pursued by two Underbottoms, an ogre, and a line of cars that were ripping off the lot to follow him, he was *driving a car all by himself* and just wait until the others saw him!

Bump, bump, bump went the road. Truth be told, Jack was not staying entirely on it, jerking left and right as he tried to get a handle on steering. He took corners too sharply, overturned the wheel, and spent much too much time stretching to reach the pedals, lacking the time to adjust his seat. Twice he almost careened off the cliff, and he thought back to the school bus he had ridden with Booger, and the game that now, by himself, was much more deadly.

In the rear-view mirror he could see the dark

cars following him, angry and close. How could he lose them? There was only one path down the mountain, and they were already close to overtaking him.

One of the cars rammed Jack from behind, and for a moment, he lost control.

He pressed on the brakes, turning his wheel as the car skidded sideways, precariously close to the edge.

But the son of Death was not to be done away with so easily. He regained control just as the front wheel slipped off the side, and though his heart leapt to his throat, in another few seconds the car was back on the road, the car behind him accelerating again for another bump.

There would come a time in Jack's life when he would be skilled at car chases and evasion maneuvers, but, unfortunately, this was not it. He knew he needed to end the chase, and quickly. But where could he go? He wasn't even sure if he was headed in the right direction, toward the Golden Bloods.

The car behind him drew nearer, and Jack accelerated.

As he rounded the next curve, he saw a little opening of a dirt path and made a split-second decision.

The car's wheels protested as Jack jerked them sideways, crashing through a wooden gate and onto the dirt trail. First one, then two of the cars in pursuit tore by him, too surprised to follow. Jack turned his attention forward, slowing down as the path narrowed. Soon the branches of the forest were closing in around him, and the road tapered into a narrow footpath. He would have to make the rest of his escape on foot.

Jack slammed his foot on the brakes, but too late: the car went careening into a thicket of branches, and only by spinning his wheel at the last moment did he avoid crashing into the nearest tree. He let out a cry of triumph at this narrow miss, his chest pressing against the seatbelt that now gripped him. Once, twice, the car spun around, until it came to a gasping stop just off the narrow trail. Jack remembered to put the car in park as the front began to steam. Well, he thought, all in all not bad for a first effort.

He was about to hop out of the car when he saw the papers.

They had fluttered down when he had been scrounging in the glove box for the spare key. It was not the words that caught his eye, not at first, but the two color photographs.

One was Nadine.

The other was Jack.

SON OF DEATH, the text underneath read, followed by a great many instructions about apprehending him. His mouth went dry, and just as he was about to turn to Nadine's page, the lights of another car flashed on. Someone had followed him.

He grabbed the papers and stuffed them in his—Nadine's—jacket pocket, before jumping out of the car and tearing across the woods. Maybe I'll become a fugitive hermit, he thought, wandering the forest and taking down the Fixers and Magical Creatures one by one.

He really could be a foolish little boy sometimes.

"There! Get him!" the men in sunglasses shouted, parking their cars and leaping out with guns at the ready. Over their radio, Crusty was swearing at them, in what was his version of a motivational speech.

"Dead or alive!" Crusty finally finished. "Do you hear me? He won't mess this up for us! DEAD OR ALIVE."

CHAPTER 23

Professor Blunderbunn had a conscience. It was a troublesome thing, and for a very long while he tried to pretend that it really didn't exist at all. You see, if he didn't have a conscience, he wouldn't have to worry about forgetting his mother's birthday (every year! Even when he marked the calendar with a reminder!), or about the fact that he sometimes crossed the street without waiting for the "walk" signal, or about his habit of sampling candies at the store even when the angry signs warned there were *NO SAMPLES ALLOWED.*

Still, he always tried to outsmart his conscience. For instance, he told himself that he had a responsibility—nay, a duty—to take his rickety plane and flee the town, because a mind such as his should not be wasted on a troll's supper. Think of all of his students!

How devastated they would be to find out he could no longer give them virtual homework! How crestfallen to discover there would be no virtual final exam!

So he told himself, and he was halfway across the state before he finally gave up and admitted that he could not just abandon the town. A man like him—smart, clever, prepared—was pretty much the town's only hope of survival, after all.

And so, after refueling at a gas station, Professor Blunderbunn went back up into the sky, complimenting himself on his much improved aviation skills. He flew low over the town as he returned, seeing the destruction that the Magical Creatures had wrought, from broken windows to blazing buildings to trampled flowers in the town park. He saw a group of fairies dressing the town's statue—a regal soldier on horseback—in a woman's scarf and underthings and sighed.

But the people were gone.

"Curious," muttered Professor Blunderbunn to himself, confident that his mind could work out the riddle. He snapped his fingers a moment later, temporarily losing control of the plane in the process.

"Well!" he said, when he had recovered. "Didn't we get a pamphlet about this, Mittens? Evacuation, no doubt. Somewhere up in the mountains."

Mittens mewed her assent.

"To the mountains we go, then!" said Professor

Blunderbunn, resolving that he would offer the use of his plane to a senior military official, who could use it on some reconnaissance or other deadly mission. Professor Blunderbunn, meanwhile, would sip tea or hot chocolate with the other refugees and bask in the glow of his heroic decision to return.

Except, he couldn't see the evacuation building as he flew overhead. One, two passes he made, and saw a curious line of buses chugging along the opposite side of the mountain. But still no rescue center.

Professor Blunderbunn's stomach grumbled. He was trying his best to leave his cookies for the afternoon, for his mother had drilled into him that it was not proper to have cookies before lunchtime. But, he figured, it was an emergency, after all, and what harm would a little snack do? He had added some nuts to the cookies, and that made them healthy.

Professor Blunderbunn picked a clearing and landed clumsily.

"Well!" he said, as Mittens hissed and jumped off his lap, cowering by his feet. Her hackles were raised, and she swiped at his hand as he reached down to comfort her. "A little shaky, but a very difficult maneuver, after all. Now, let's have a few of those cookies, yes? And maybe ask for directions. There's a fellow."

He shielded his eyes and peered down the front

of his plane, where a boy was racing toward him. It looked like—but no, that couldn't be—

The boy's arms waved frantically.

"You again!" Professor Blunderbunn said irritably, leaning out of the cockpit. "Didn't I already save you once? Hmph! There are other people who need my help, you know."

"They're coming!" the boy shouted. "Start the engines! Start the plane!" And the nerve of the fellow— he jumped right back onto Professor Blunderbunn's plane, and gripped the wing as if ready for flight.

"Who...what in the name...?"

A badly beaten-up black car roared into the clearing, followed by a few men in sunglasses and dark gear. They spun, spotted Professor Blunderbunn's plane, and raced forward.

"Fixers!" the professor cried, his heart pounding. "Hold on, boy!"

He started up the plane again, ignoring the scent of smoke as the gears ground and the poor, tired engines tried to rev up once more. The old plane finally rambled forward, just as one of the Fixers aimed his gun and shot at them.

"F! F minus!" Professor Blunderbunn swore, clearing the tops of the trees. The plane wobbled under the unbalanced weight. "Hold on tight!"

Half an hour later, after Professor Blunderbunn had made a clumsy crash landing on the next mountain over, the two new allies discussed their course of action over some of the professor's smushed cookies.

"Fixers," Professor Blunderbunn muttered. "Fixers! We're in trouble, indeed."

Jack explained everything he knew, wishing the professor would pay a little less attention to his kitten and a little more attention to the dangerous situation at hand. But though the professor listened to Jack's tale of Crusty and the ogre and shook his head when Jack described the nefarious schemes of the villain to divide the Black and Golden Bloods, he did not seem in any particular hurry to sort things out.

"It happens all the time," Professor Blunderbunn said. "All the time. When you get to be my age, Jack, you'll see that people use any excuse they can to divide people. The stranger, the better!"

"But we have to save the Golden Bloods!" Jack burst, thinking of Nadine. He remembered the papers, and scrounged to find them—but the plane ride must have ripped them from his pocket, for he found only crumbs and dust.

"You can't be sure they're in any danger."

"Crusty said as much!"

Professor Blunderbunn chewed on his bottom lip. "You know, my dear boy, there is a long, involved political and social history of the Fixers? You might find it interesting. When they started, you see, they were dead set against any sort of mixing of—"

"Professor!"

"What?"

"There's no time!"

Well, thought the professor, there was *always* time for a history lesson. But he grumpily agreed that if lives were in danger he could put it off for a bit.

"I think our first course of action is to notify the proper authorities," said Professor Blunderbunn.

"You mean the Fixers?"

"Oh! Hmm, yes, that does throw a wrench in things. Let me think."

"Professor…"

"We could always ask the federal investigators. They specialize in crime, but perhaps…"

"Professor—"

"Ah! No, the Bureau of Magical Creature Control. They'll want to know about this, certainly. And they're in an entirely different branch than the Fixers— in fact, there's a bit of political rivalry there, if you know what I mean…"

"Professor!"

Professor Blunderbunn huffed and looked up at

Jack. "What?"

"I need you to take me to the Golden Bloods."

"But—"

"I'll rescue them myself."

Professor Blunderbunn had never heard such a terrible idea in his life. It was ridiculous! It was foolish! It was an outrage!

"That's ridiculous! It's foolish! It's an outrage!" he snapped.

But Jack was resolute. "I have to save Nadine."

"Young love!" the professor said, throwing up his hands and ignoring the horrified gape of Jack, who blushed deeply. "Well, *I* for one do not support this mission. You must go through the proper channels to get things done."

Jack listened to the professor's excuses as patiently as he could, waiting to point out that Professor Blunderbunn had just effected a marvelous, illegal escape from the Fixers, and could certainly not be as concerned with proper channels as he was pretending. But in the end the professor tired himself out, threw up his hands, and asked, "Do you know how to use a parachute?"

"Yes," said Jack, who didn't.

"Good. Climb aboard, then! I'll drop you off, yes? On my way to discuss this unpleasant situation with the proper authorities."

CHAPTER 24

And where, you are saying, are all of the Grim Reapers?

Oh, do not worry. There will be more.

One of them watched Professor Blunderbunn's plane with interest, following as Jack strapped the parachute to his back and climbed onto the wing. Mittens caught sight of the Reaper and hissed, but Professor Blunderbunn, oblivious, told her to be a good kitty and please be quiet.

The Reaper—a trainee, understand—followed the plane as it rumbled across the clearing and took off, trying to keep pace beneath it, scrambling to remember its transport spells. It fell behind and slunk back off to the waiting room, where its manager had quite a long talk with it about professional standards and incompetency.

The other, smarter, older Reapers were all moving toward where the Golden Bloods were being kept.

By now, Jack was an accustomed traveler on Professor Blunderbunn's rickety plane.

He was not, however, prepared for parachuting.

"It is very simple—you jump and pull the cord," the professor had told Jack, as they were suiting up for their final flight. It had all seemed easy and logical on the ground, but now, as Jack peered over the wing at the changing landscape beneath, he became rather queasy, and wondered just how reliable an old sack on his shoulders would be at keeping him alive.

Professor Blunderbunn circled for some time, searching for the hideout where the Golden Bloods had been taken. Along the way, Jack caught sight of some of the destruction of his town, as well as the crumbled wall that bordered the reserve. Was that a giant smashing through the school? And what were those little creatures dancing about the streets, swinging from the stoplights?

Hours and hours it seemed they flew, until the professor began to circle around a mountaintop, one just a few miles away from the evacuation center. Jack felt another knot form in his stomach as he looked down at the razor-sharp rocks and pointed trees below.

Professor Blunderbunn waved at Jack from his safe and snug cockpit. He pointed down at a small white building with a few vans parked outside and gave Jack a thumbs-up. Jack, keeping a tight grip on the wing's handle, did not return it.

Two, three more times they circled, as Jack tried to work up the courage to jump. Now that he thought about it, had the professor given him the right pack? Hadn't he hesitated, muttering something about faulty levers and repairs?

Then the plane dipped sideways, and Jack tumbled off the wing.

"There, there," Professor Blunderbunn comforted Mittens, as the kitten dug its claws into the professor's calf. "He was getting cold feet. Just needed a little nudge." Still, the professor looked anxiously to where the boy had fallen, trying to spot the gold fabric of the parachute amongst the trees. "I'm sure he made it," said the professor nervously.

And he turned the plane about and went to notify the proper authorities.

Jack tumbled over and over in the air. Have you ever been on a roller coaster? Imagine that you are on the world's longest downward slope, except you are about to die and your best friend is not screaming with delight beside you. That is how Jack felt.

He reached up and tugged on his shoulders, pulling every bit of fabric he could reach, too afraid to remember where, precisely, the ripcord was. Only by chance did his fingers snag the handle at the last second, and the great gold parachute went *PFFT!* as it opened.

Jack breathed a sigh of relief.

And then he crashed into the trees.

Later, Jack would always remember his first experience with a parachute and laugh at his own fool-ishness. But Jack was not laughing then, as the gold fabric clung to the treetops, and the cords that attached to Jack's pack became hopelessly tangled amongst the trees' branches.

A few birds cackled as Jack struggled to free himself, though a sleepy owl opened one eye and told them to mind their own business. A fox padded over to see what all the commotion was about and had a good laugh with the mole later that day during their evening tea.

"Like this!" the fox would say, moving his limbs like an upside-down spider. The mole, nearly blind, would laugh anyway, because he was a terrible suck-up.

Soon Jack managed to get his arms around a

sturdy branch and from there haul himself up to a sitting position. He tore off the parachute and tossed it into the trees, where it landed on an indignant crow (one of those that had been laughing at him, in fact) and tumbled to the ground.

Well, he thought, *off to a promising start!*

High up in the trees, Jack could spot exactly where he had to go. The white building was no more than a football field away, and now Jack could see a few sunglass- and suit-wearing men hurrying about outside, speaking into their phones. A dark car pulled up, and a short man and large figure got out. It was too far to see properly, but Jack already knew who they were: Crusty and the ogre.

Time was running out.

CHAPTER 25

Deborah had first told Jack about his father when he was five years old. "Old enough," she had told him menacingly, "to keep a Secret." Jack, who was too young to really care much about not having his father around, had listened with mild interest as Deborah explained about special families, and Magical Creatures, and Black and Gold Bloodlines. Halfway through, he had asked her if he could go to the park.

"No interruptions!" Deborah snapped. She took a long swig of coffee and shut off the television, which was playing a cartoon featuring a dancing bear with dreams of joining the ballet. "I'm going to tell you who your father is, Jack, and I need you to keep it a Secret."

Jack nodded. In those days, he had always wanted

a deep, dark Secret. All the best heroes had them.

"Your father is...Death."

Jack remembered feeling disappointed. When his mother had explained about trolls and elves and giants, he had been hoping his father would be among those. Wouldn't it just be marvelous to have the strength of a troll, or the speed of an elf, or the appetite of a giant?

"Alright," Jack had said.

"Do you have any questions for me?"

Five-year-old Jack blinked up at Deborah and shrugged.

Now, ten-year-old Jack had quite a few questions. It was just too late to ask them.

After a lifetime of being told just how dangerous the outside world was, Nadine was sharper than most. And she was among the first to realize that the Golden Bloods had walked into a trap.

"Well!" all the others said, patting each other on the shoulders and sighing with relief, "so glad to be out of there! You know, with *those* people."

"Quite right," their companions would say. "Nasty business, holing us up with the likes of them!" They had forgotten, by this time, that they had lived most of their lives as the neighbors and friends and even family of the Black Bloods.

But Nadine kept an eye on their drivers, and then their guides, and then the overly helpful men in sunglasses who ushered them into an identical gymnasium from the one they had just left—except that this one was completely empty.

"Oh, we don't expect you to sleep on *cots!*" one of the men in sunglasses exclaimed.

"Quite right, quite right," muttered the Golden Bloods. They were assured that they would each be receiving access to a private bedroom and bathroom upstairs, once all of the keys were sorted out. Nadine frowned. From what she had seen of the outside of the building, there *wasn't* an upstairs. She tried to point this out to the woman beside her, who hushed her and told her to let the adults handle things.

Nadine wished Jack were there. It had been nice having a friend, even if only for a little while.

She thought of her father, away on his business trip. It was probably for the best. No doubt he would have a heart attack if he knew that Nadine was in any danger. He always thought she couldn't take care of herself.

Nadine glanced toward where the men in sunglasses had gathered, pretending to talk casually as they guarded the door.

Well, she thought, this time she would have to

handle things.

Nadine slipped away from the crowd and had just made her way to the back stairwell (which led *down,* not *up*), when a scream ripped through the air. The lights in the gymnasium went out.

Jack heard the scream just as he was approaching. A chill went through him and he ducked behind a nearby tree as the lights inside went dark.

Not too late to turn back, a cowardly voice whispered inside him. He pushed it down and peeked back around the trees, heart thumping. That was when he saw them.

He blinked a few times and rubbed his eyes, not sure he trusted what he was seeing. Grim Reapers, emerging by twos and threes from the woods, headed toward the gymnasium. And mixed in among them, seemingly oblivious to their presence, were more men in sunglasses, ushering along trolls and giants and ogres and the occasional dwarf, saying, "Yes, a *delicious* meal inside, refreshments provided, step this way, please…"

Jack's mouth had gone dry. He had never even seen a Grim Reaper before, but he knew—deep in his bones—what they were. And he had the strange sensation that they would recognize him, too.

And that was when he realized that the Fixers did not intend for any of the Golden Bloods to make it out alive.

Jack moved quickly. He went around to the other side of the building and tiptoed across the brush-covered earth, his eye on the back door. How he was going to save all those people, he didn't know— but he needed help. He needed Nadine.

And maybe, just maybe, someone else as well.

He heard another scream as he tugged at the door handle. A troll growl reached him, and Jack remembered poor Booger. He wiped sweat from his forehead and tugged again, trying to think through his fear. But his worries clouded his thoughts, and instead of stepping back to form a better plan, he only pulled harder and harder and harder, shivering as another scream followed.

Jack felt a chill come over him.

He looked up and caught sight of a Reaper.

CHAPTER 26

Ahem. Grim Reaper here, a pleasure to meet you. Personal guard of Jack Hallows, the son of Death. And chronicler of this extraordinary story.

I considered chastising the boy to start. After all, when you are the son of Death, you do not go around exposing yourself to all sorts of dangers. Did he think, I wanted to ask, that because he was the son of Death, he would receive some sort of special treatment? Perhaps get whisked away from the line of spirits and sent back to the living? Ha!

But his father had not employed me to lecture the boy, and so against my better judgment, I remained silent.

"Am I about to die?" Jack asked. He had gone a very pale shade of white.

Oh, heavens! I thought. He thinks I am *his* Reaper, come to take him away. I began to laugh, which manifested itself as a sort of guttural churning that only made the boy go even whiter. I shook my head.

"Did my father send you?" he whispered.

Again I shook my head. I really wasn't even supposed to interact with the young fellow, but desperate times called for desperate measures. I couldn't let the boy just waltz into the gymnasium and expose himself to the corporate party of the year. Have you ever seen a Grim Reaper lose his reaping license? A terrible affair for all involved.

The boy straightened up. "Well, perhaps—perhaps you can help me then. With this door."

I snorted. I would have told him that, though he might be the son of Death, he did not sign *my* paychecks, but just then two more of my brethren appeared, talking excitedly at the edge of the clearing. Jack glanced over at them, and I followed his gaze, frowning.

Oh, my. Grim Reapers within and without—was there no safe place? I suppose I should have prevented the boy from going there in the first place, but how was I to know that the idiot Blunderbunn would manage to find the second evacuation center? Pure luck, really, and I had also busied myself beating back the Reaper that stood under Jack's tree, hoping a good fall would earn him a much-needed credit on his scorecard.

I bent down low, until I came face to face with Jack. He flinched but, to his credit, did not move back. There are not many who, when they see us, can manage that. Then again, Jack was the only one who *could* see us without an imminent death.

"You," I said, struggling to make my voice smaller, more earthly, "will need to be very careful. This is not your war."

Jack's eyes widened. "Nadine—"

"Your father," I said sternly, "would not approve of that friendship."

"Can't he help me? Can't he...call off his Reapers?"

Oh, the horror! The foolish simplicity of such a suggestion. And where would the spirits go then? Just wander the forest like a bunch of banshees and ghosts? I recoiled at the thought.

"Not his war," I repeated again. The foolishness of youth! Well, there was not much else to be done. Neither out nor in was safe, and sometimes, that's just the way of the world. I reached forth my hand, pressing my fingers against the cold lock. It clicked, and in the next moment, the door opened. I let my form dissolve back into the air.

Jack was shaken; never before had he spoken to one of his father's Reapers, and he was still not entirely convinced that yours truly was not about to leap on him from behind and drag him to the underworld (the absurdity of some people's conceptions of my work!). But he pushed through the door and passed through, feeling a little shiver of recognition as his fingers connected with the last remnants of my spell. The old, ancient magic was awakening in him, too.

Very soon, I thought to myself, babysitting is not going to be quite so easy as before.

Jack slithered through the back halls, giving wide berth to any Reapers he saw walking through. They saluted him as he passed, but he was much too distracted to take notice.

"Nadine!" he whispered. "Nadine!"

And, quite fortuitously, Nadine showed up.

CHAPTER 27

Do you want a bloody description of that unfortunate slaughter? I thought as much.

Many a man and woman were gobbled right up.

Bones were snapped and cracked and noshed and nibbled.

Tears fell and throats screamed, but it made not one little glint of difference. The creatures, you see, were not in a forgiving mood. While a few were grateful for the privacy and solitude of the creature reserve, the vast majority felt it a supreme insult to their status.

"Why, the next day they'll be calling it a zoo!" some had said, as Magical Creature Control herded them into the reserve.

They would have been just as happy to take out their revenge on the Black Bloods, understand, but beggars can't be choosers, and they had been all too happy to listen to Crusty place the blame for their imprisonment on the Golden Bloods. The trolls never liked the elves anyway, and the ogres found the fairies mischievous in all the worst sorts of ways.

Plus, they were all fairly hungry.

But enough of that. You do not want to hear about the full bellies of the ogres, or the victory dances of the dwarves, or the greedy Reapers that battled to take away the spirits of the fallen (quotas were coming up, you see). It was all very unpleasant work, and if you are lucky, nothing so unfortunate will ever happen to you.

You will be interested, however, in the extraordinary events that happened next.

"Jack!" cried Nadine.

"Nadine!" cried Jack.

They were delighted to see one another and quite relieved, too, though they skipped over the pleasantries and got right down to business.

"It was a trap," Nadine said, her eyes glowing.

"I know," said Jack. "I came to save you."

Nadine blushed, and then Jack blushed, and then the two of them remembered they were in mortal danger and did not have time for embarrassment.

"Come on," Jack said. "We have to save them."

"Do you have a plan?" Nadine followed Jack as he began to run down the hallway, back toward the open gymnasium.

"Not yet."

"Jack—" Nadine grabbed his elbow, trembling as she heard another victorious ogre roar. "You're safe. You're a Black Blood, aren't you? I'm...I'm Golden. My mother—"

"You can tell me later."

"But it's dangerous. You don't know—"

"Later," Jack said, seeing how much Nadine's Secret tore at her. He had never been particularly troubled by his own, despite knowing how rare a Secret it was. A tingling of curiosity went through him, but he pushed it back down. There were lives to save, after all. The Secrets could be kept, at least for a little while longer.

As Nadine and Jack crept to the edge of the gymnasium, they found the fallen body of a troll (trampled by a pair of overeager ogres) and the stunned, gurgling body of a sleepy giant. Jack took an ugly knife from the troll, and Nadine pulled out the giant's pocket knife, which for her served as an appropriately-sized sword. Jack wanted to say something about how girls shouldn't have to fight, but he was glad of the help and so just asked Nadine if she was sure she was ready.

"Yes," Nadine said.

Never had Jack imagined that his quiet, sheltered neighbor would be such a ready ally in a Magical Creature fight. Even Booger, Jack was sure, would have taken a little convincing.

They opened the door to the gymnasium and rushed in.

CHAPTER 28

The battle was, at first, a haze of impressions for Jack.

An ugly, thick troll arm swatting toward him.

An evil ogre's grin gaping as pink lips lifted to reveal yellowed teeth.

A hysterical woman crying, "Where is my private suite?" as a young man dragged her back to safety.

It was all very confusing, and frightening, and obvious that a few good blows of an ugly troll knife would not set everything right. Nadine and Jack stayed close together, and soon managed to make their way around the side of the gymnasium, where they rescued a crying child from a slow-moving dwarf and pulled an ogre away from a screaming, hysterical teenage girl.

"He bit my shoe! He bit my shoe!" the girl cried, but Jack and Nadine had already moved on.

They moved into a very uneasy rhythm, Jack pointing out their missions and Nadine grimly following behind. Jack would rush the assailant, not giving his cowardice time to yawn and stretch and protest, and Nadine would follow, disposing of the creature with a few expert swipes of her knife. Jack was pretty sure that she had practiced this type of stuff before.

Something funny began to happen to Jack as he worked. He felt a roaring inside of himself, a distant stir deep inside his chest. It seemed to him that the monsters knew instinctively to avoid him, and that his touch—just sometimes, just a little—seemed to stun some of them, or at least have more power than he had expected. Maybe it was all of those push-ups in gym.

As he was busy fighting Magical Creatures and saving lives, of course he didn't have much time to analyze these sensations. Or to think about all of the very troublesome things they might mean for him later.

"Pay attention!" Nadine snapped at him, during one moment where he almost—almost—began thinking about it.

"Make sure he doesn't use them," a Reaper whispered to me. Not just any Reaper—a Head Reaper. I shuddered and nodded, and said a quick prayer that the boy would not be so foolish. *Not here,* I thought. *Not like this. You're not ready.*

The gymnasium was too crowded, too chaotic. There was no way Nadine and Jack could save everyone. Indeed, it was too late for a great many of the Golden Bloods. Just as Jack was about to point this out to Nadine and suggest they retreat, a giant lunged at them.

Nadine screamed and dropped her sword.

Jack stumbled backwards and swung wildly with his knife.

The giant cackled and picked them both up, one in each enormous fist. He was a middling giant, twice as tall as a full-grown man, with a mangy beard and a pair of bright green eyes.

"Jack!" Nadine gasped, struggling against the giant's thick fingers, which were squeezing her tighter and tighter around the middle. "I...have to tell you..."

The gymnasium shook. Jack, his vision dulling as the giant squeezed tighter, wondered if it was another giant come to finish them all off.

Jack thought of his mother, who had tried to get him to promise to stay safely in the other rescue center.

Jack thought of Booger, who had been so cruelly eaten at the start of these horrors, who deserved justice that Jack couldn't deliver.

Jack thought of Urkel, who much more deserved to be in a giant's death grip.

Jack thought of Professor Blunderbunn, probably eating cookies and flying over the ocean by now.

Well, Jack thought, as he lifted his weak hand, still gripping the knife, and brought it down one last time, I suppose I'll get to meet my father after all.

The knife plunged into the giant's fingers just as the gymnasium shook again. A great many things happened at once.

The Grim Reapers, realizing their main work was coming to an end, scurried from the hall, quite a few with sour looks on their faces.

The Black Blood creatures roared and howled, some of them with a stomachache, as the gymnasium shook and tilted. The windows rattled as a great wind swept in.

The Golden Blood humans fled or hid, whichever was easier.

The giant holding Nadine and Jack howled as Jack's knife connected with its thumb, and dropped its quarry.

Jack's mother pulled up in a reinforced car, a few nervous guards from Magical Creature Control trembling in the backseat.

"My word," she said, as she watched the flight of the Magical Creatures. "She's here."

One of the Magical Creature Control workers fainted in fear.

The gymnasium continued to shake. Nadine crawled away from where the giant was tottering, threatening to fall and squash them. Jack groaned, sat up, and soon managed to pull himself to his feet, rushing over to help Nadine just as the giant's feet gave way and he landed on the floor with a *SMASH.*

"We have to get out!" Nadine shouted, but she had to repeat it twice before Jack heard her over the roar of the floor splitting beneath them. Apparently quite a few Magical Creatures had the same thought, for soon they were all making a mad dash for the exit, thrusting Golden Bloods and smaller creatures aside.

Jack grabbed Nadine's hand and pulled her back, toward the hallway they had come through. They battled the surge of creatures moving in the opposite direction, ducking and diving and jumping until they pushed through the back door and sprinted through the hall.

"What's going *on?*" Jack shouted over his shoulder, for Nadine had begun to shake.

"I've never— I've never—" she started, but then

they had pushed themselves out of the hallway and into the blinding sunlight, where a whole zoo of Magical Creatures and dazed Golden Bloods were wandering.

Jack's jaw dropped open.

Before them, the forest had changed. No, the whole world had changed. The trees had grown to three times their size and turned soot black, their tops pointed like spears. The ground was split with rivulets of red, including one line that ran right through the gymnasium and rumbled ominously. Even the sky overhead had changed, clouds cottony white against the deep blue of the sky, the sun a blinding bulb of white.

"What's going on?" Jack asked. He noticed that all Grim Reapers had magically disappeared, and for one terrifying moment he wondered if his father would rear up from the creases of the earth and declare that they were all going to be spirited off to the under-world.

He looked left and right for some escape and saw, with a stab of guilt even through all of his fear, a stocky figure outside a dark Magical Creatures Control van. "My mom," Jack said, his mouth dry. Some of the creatures rushed into the trees, not pausing to look back. "My mom is here."

"Mine too," Nadine whispered.

Nadine and Jack looked at one another. The

ground trembled, the sky roared. A man running past shouted for them to run for their lives, if they valued them.

"I shouldn't have come," Nadine said, shivering. "You shouldn't have come. We're all in danger."

Jack decided there wasn't time to point out that they would be in danger no matter who was coming where. Instead he asked, "Who's your mother?"

Nadine blushed, even as the ground split wider beneath them. She had so enjoyed having a friend. Did it have to come to an end so soon?

"My father is Death," Jack said, his voice low. "It's a Secret, like yours."

Tears came to Nadine's eyes. "Mine is Earth," Nadine said. "Mother Earth."

The ground trembled and cracked wider, throwing the children down.

CHAPTER 29

Oh, please! you're saying. *Mother Earth? How silly! What a ridiculous story! A mere legend!*

Well, you're wrong, and quite rude, too. Do you think Mother Earth is beyond the childbearing age? Do you think she is called Mother Earth because her first name is Mother?

Why I bother wasting my time defending her is beyond me. Certainly her relationship with Death has never been cordial. But I do so hate ignorance.

Jack knew right away that Nadine told the truth, and what's more, that it was a very dangerous one.

"*Mother Earth?*" he repeated, his eyes wide.

Nadine nodded.

But they had no more time for discussion, for the transformed trees began to teeter near the clearing and were soon falling down amongst the panicking crowd. Jack and Nadine sprinted to their right, dashing through the chaos all around them. They stopped only when their legs could go no farther, and they bent over their knees, drawing in quick, ragged breaths.

They were so exhausted that neither of them heard the rustle of whispers at the edge of Mother Nature's horrid spell, nor noticed the golden-eyed Guardian—a real snoot I had had the misfortune of meeting here and there over the centuries—creep closer to Nadine and give me a hard look.

"I'm sorry," Nadine said, and though I would have apologized if my parent was Mother Earth, too, Jack only looked confused.

"There's nothing to be sorry about."

Nadine looked like she might cry. Jack looked like he might start running again. "I guess," she said, her voice breaking, "we can't be friends any longer."

"What?"

"I said I guess—"

"Why would you say that? Of course we can."

Nadine looked up at him, not daring to hope. "Of course we can," Jack repeated. "We're friends now, aren't we?" He didn't wait for her to answer, which was wise, because Nadine was hastily wiping away a tear. "Then we'll stay friends. No matter who our parents are."

Oh, I hated it. I wanted to run out and shake Jack, and say, *obviously you can't just say you'll be friends with such a girl as that, not with my performance review coming up!* But what was I to do? The golden-eyed Guardian, keeping well back, looked similarly troubled, and we put aside our enmity for one moment to share a long glance of horror and annoyance. An alliance! This was not...it could not... well, perhaps I didn't have to put it in my report, not yet...

"Alright," Nadine said, making an impressive show of pretending she had not been close to crying at all, and drawing herself up as she pushed her shoulders back. She extended one hand to Jack. "Friends, then."

"Friends."

I wasn't sure if they noticed the faint buzz of electricity as their hands touched. Everything was awakening now. It was too late to put a stop to it.

"Jack!" called a familiar voice. "Jack!"

Nadine and Jack turned and tromped back through the forest, joining a none-too-pleased Deborah as a swarm of other Golden Bloods began piling into the Magical Creature Control van, demanding that someone—anyone—drive them away to safety.

"Well," said Deborah, who would not waste time chastising Jack for something that could no longer be changed (though she resolved to have a nice long talk with Jack about the word "obedience" later). "It seems we're in a bit of a pickle."

This was coming to be a typical state for them, Jack thought.

"What's your mom doing?" Jack shouted, but both Deborah and Nadine hushed him, looking around for eavesdroppers. *"You* know?" he asked his mother.

"Mr. Jang and I...we've exchanged words," she said, her face hardening. "Nadine, do you know how to stop this?"

"I've never spoken to her," Nadine said anxiously, keeping her voice low. "My father wouldn't— he said it wasn't—"

"Quite right," Deborah said, sighing. "But evidently she was feeling a little protective today. But not to worry! Your father is on his way. I've made sure of that."

More trees came crashing down over the clearing, and the great red cracks in the earth began to spurt what looked like molten lava.

At first, Jack didn't hear the rumble overhead— or at least, he thought it was just part of the great cracking of the earth beneath him. But then his mother gasped, and Nadine let out a small yelp, and a shadow fell over the clearing.

Professor Blunderbunn's plane passed low

overhead and came to a stuttering stop a few feet into the forest. The front end was smoking.

"My dad!" Nadine said, pointing at the tall, dark-haired figure that clambered down from one of the wings. The others were too panicked to pay the plane much mind. The creatures were busy running into the forest, while nearby, Golden Bloods were pressing Magical Creature Control to take them away in their vans. Jack thought he caught sight of Crusty, huddled together with a few men in sunglasses and one ugly ogre in a sundress, until they disappeared into a dark car and, with a last sinister glance at the gymnasium, drove off.

Mr. Jang hurried over, his suit rumpled and his hair sticking up in all directions. "Nadine!" he said, and an apology was on Nadine's lips when Mr. Jang collapsed to his knees and wrapped her in his arms, pulling her into a fierce embrace.

Deborah cleared her throat. "Now," she said, "would be a very good time to leave."

"How do you know Professor Blunderbunn?" Jack asked, as Mr. Jang motioned for them all to run toward the smoking plane. Mr. Jang gave him a cold once-over, as if to say, *I bet this is all your fault.* Deborah put a protective arm around Jack's shoulders.

"We just met," Mr. Jang growled, which was a lie that will have to be explained at another time.

CHAPTER 30

What is there left to tell? Only a lifetime of things, but we will have to settle for a few. Nadine, Mr. Jang, Deborah, and Jack all escaped. The authorities finally started to act with authority. Arrests were made and creatures were recaptured—though just as many scuttled off into the forest to bide their time. Still, the parents had had quite enough risks for one day and were more than ready to take the authorities' suggestion that they all "take a nice little holiday" until things had calmed down.

Nadine, Mr. Jang, Deborah, and Jack all rode the wings of Professor Blunderbunn's plane to a remote stretch of farmland that the professor claimed belonged to an old friend...until his loud, corpulent Aunt Janie came trotting out and threw her meaty arms around him, insisting that they all stay for rhubarb pie and tea.

"It's been so long since you've visited, Artie!" Aunt Janie said later that night, as she made them all fried chicken and potatoes. "And you have friends now!"

"We're not—" Mr. Jang began, but Deborah loudly complimented Aunt Janie on her fried green beans.

Over dessert, Mr. Jang listened to Deborah, Jack, and Nadine tell the tale of the escaped Magical Creatures, with the occasional interjection from Professor Blunderbunn. Mr. Jang listened gravely, shaking his head when Crusty was mentioned, and again when the Golden Bloods were separated, and yet again when the children had found themselves in the final confrontation. He and Deborah shared a worried look.

"I had hoped we would be beyond all this," Mr. Jang said. "If they're determined to look into heritage—"

"You're not the only one with a Secret to keep," said Deborah, pointing her fork at him. Aunt Janie asked if anyone would like any more pie.

"They're trying to start something," Mr. Jang said. "The Fixers! I thought they were gotten rid of years ago."

"They just learned to be a lot quieter."

"If people believe them..."

"After this disaster? I should hope not! Didn't you see the police there? They'll take care of them."

"That strikes me as hopelessly naïve, Deborah."

"You strike me as hopelessly annoying, Mr. Jang." They argued for a bit more about how many Fixers had escaped and how big the network could be, until Aunt Janie loudly told them to eat more pie. The adults simmered down, but not before Deborah muttered, "It's the same old trouble, always being stirred up."

Deborah and Mr. Jang continued discussing politics and history and other things that had little relevance and thus little interest for Nadine and Jack. They were happy to be safe, and reunited, and eating rhubarb pie in a warm farmhouse away from any ogres or trolls or evil men named Crusty (or Urkel, for that matter).

Mr. Jang cleared his throat. "I suppose," he said haltingly, as if the words pained him very much, "that I should thank you for looking after my Nadine. That is, I am usually so very careful, but...I am grateful."

Jack jumped as he realized Mr. Jang was addressing him. Blushing, he looked quickly toward Nadine, who was picking at the tablecloth. He muttered something that might have been "you're welcome" or "more pie."

"We can't protect them forever," Deborah said

with a sigh.

"Indeed," said Mr. Jang. "In fact, I fear the time for that has already passed."

And then, when they had all eaten more dessert, and the adults began to split a bottle of brandy that Aunt Janie brought out, and Professor Blunderbunn had excused himself to tend to his still-smoking plane, Nadine and Jack resumed the tale of their adventures. They glossed over some dangers and accentuating others, telling of the creatures they defeated, the children they defended, and the giant that had almost done them in at the end. Mr. Jang's face oscillated between red and white, while Deborah hiccupped and repeated at various intervals that they were "foolish and lucky."

"Do you think school will be canceled?" Jack asked, and Nadine and Jack spent a hopeful few minutes waiting for Aunt Janie to look up the news. Reinforcements had been called in to round up the Magical Creatures, and neighboring towns had pitched in to help rebuild the wall (more out of fear than any sort of generosity). Things were not yet back to normal, but all signs pointed in that direction.

There was no mention of Crusty, and the Fixers received only the most passing of references—a few arrests here and there, and a general smug attitude of "all is well, we've got everything handled."

"We'll be out of the woods soon," Deborah said, and the small party—save for smiling Aunt Janie, who trotted off to check on her tea—shuddered to remember the scene earlier that day.

"Was she angry?" Nadine asked shyly, looking up at her father. "Mother...Mother Earth?"

Mr. Jang winced. "No, my dear. She was just... well, you're so young, and..."

Deborah glanced from Mr. Jang to Jack to Nadine. "I suppose," she said, "there can't be any Secrets between us."

"Not many," corrected Mr. Jang.

"Not many." Deborah turned toward Jack. "Do you know what happens to the offspring of Mother Earth, Jack?"

Jack shook his head. Mr. Jang frowned but did not interrupt. Nadine blushed and ducked her head.

"Well, I'll put it this way. The first troll, the first elf, the first fairy—all of them had the same mother. The same mother as her." She nodded toward Nadine.

It took Jack a few moments to process this. It is not every day, after all, that you learn that your new best friend may just be the start to a new magical race. But when it clicked—

"Cool!"

A wide grin split his face, and Nadine looked up at him in wonder. Soon an answering smile bloomed on hers.

"So what are you?" Jack asked.

"What do you mean?"

"What Magical Creature? I guess giants and fairies and goblins are all taken."

Nadine shrugged. "I don't know yet. I—"

"She's not old enough," said Mr. Jang sharply. "And she's in no hurry to grow up."

Deborah harrumphed.

"What about me?" Jack asked his mother. "Do I turn into a Grim Reaper or something?"

"Heavens, no!"

Jack felt both relieved and disappointed. He spent the entire time scrubbing plates after dinner brainstorming with Nadine about what sort of creature she might become, and what sort of powers she might get. Nadine, who was used to this sort of speculation, having spent most of her nights practicing it, giggled at Jack's wild guesses and said that, soon enough, they would find out.

"And you, too!" Nadine said, still giggling, and they spent a few more minutes imagining what sort of children Death had. If Jack didn't turn into a Grim Reaper, maybe he'd be some sort of underworld guide? Perhaps a very troublesome poltergeist? Jack played along, though even he was wise enough not to mention those nagging, budding feelings he had felt during the Magical Creature battle, the ones that suggested—but no, he wouldn't even think of it.

"Time for bed!" Deborah called, and announced that they would all be spending the night at Aunt Janie's and return to town in the morning, when "hopefully things will be back to normal."

Normal. A funny word, isn't it? And one that was never to visit that town, at least in the same way, again.

And off to bed they went, to snore and slumber and sigh. And Jack would have had a peaceful night of sleep, if it weren't for the midnight phone call.

CHAPTER 31

Ring, ring.

Ring, ring.

At first, Jack wondered who would be calling Aunt Janie so late at night. Then he wondered why she wasn't picking up. Finally he wondered if anyone else was hearing the rings at all.

Jack crept from his bed, his mother snoring in the one next to him. He left the guest bedroom and padded down the dark hallway, feeling a strange sense of foreboding.

Ring, ring.

Ring, ring.

It sounds like the start of a horror film, does it not? At least, that was what Jack was thinking, as he moved into the living room. He did not know that it was the end of this book.

Jack came to the blue, egg-shaped phone and picked it up.

"Hello?" he whispered.

"My goodness!" a familiar voice said. "Doesn't anyone pick up in that house?"

It was Crusty.

Jack could have slammed the phone back down. He could have run back into the bedroom and hidden under the covers or, more sensibly, woken his mother up and warned her that Crusty knew where they were. But instead he waited, tense, for the voice to continue.

"May I please speak with Jack?"

"I'm Jack."

"Oh, wonderful!" said Crusty, his voice oily and over-polite. "Just wonderful. And how are you, Jack?"

"You tried to kill the Golden Bloods."

"Did I? I don't think so. It was the Magical Creatures that got up there."

"You blasted the wall of the reserve."

"*Blasted?* Oh, my. That sounds sinister. But tell me, Jack, do you really think it fair that we relegate those poor beings to second-class citizens? What makes humans so special, hmm?"

Jack's mind was beginning to wake up, catching up with his body.

"You killed people."

"Pfft! What do little boys know about politics?" The politeness was draining from Crusty's words. "And how many times do you think the Golden Bloods have done the same and worse to the Black? You're on our side, Jack, and you shouldn't forget it."

"There aren't any sides," Jack said, growing angry. "You made them up."

"Centuries of history would argue otherwise."

Jack thought he heard a bump and turned around, his eyes scanning the shadows of the living room behind him. "How did you know I was here?"

"Let's not worry about trivialities, hmm? The point is, dear Jack, that you have a very unusual—a *highly* unusual—father. And do you think that any of the Golden Bloods will care that you tried to help them? Hmm? Not when they find out who that father is."

"It's a Secret," Jack said, flushing.

"Oh, yes, a Secret. For now. Don't you want to know how I know? Well?"

Jack held his breath.

"Your dear father told me. Not directly, of course, through a messenger...but that is that. He knows which side is right, and it's time his son realizes it, too."

Jack thought of Crusty, and the men in sunglasses, and the ogre in a summer hat, and shook his head. There was no way that *that* side was right, not when Nadine was on the other one.

"If you don't believe me, just watch how the Golden Bloods treat you," Crusty said. "The proof is in the pudding."

"What pudding?"

"It's an expression," Crusty snapped. He took a deep breath. "I think it's high time you think about your future, Jack Hallows. We will be in touch."

The phone clicked. For a moment Jack hesitated, wondering if he should go get an adult, not realizing that he was at the point now where adults could not fix everything. *It's okay, they'll find him, too, and arrest him,* he told himself. It was nice to think so. It is very comforting to believe that your problems will be handled by the proper authorities.

So, off Jack went to bed like a sensible boy.

The next morning, Jack wondered if the phone call had been a dream. It might have been. It all seemed to have taken place in another world, and as Aunt Janie flipped flapjacks and sang nursery rhymes, he pushed it from his mind.

Mr. Jang and Deborah spent the morning on the phone, taking turns calling relatives and officials and neighbors to determine just what damage had been done and if it was safe to return.

"All good," Deborah said, as the sun rose higher in the sky. She kissed Jack's head. He winced and glanced at Nadine to make sure she hadn't seen. "We can go home this afternoon."

"So they got all the creatures?" Jack asked. "They're back in the reserve?"

Deborah and Mr. Jang exchanged a glance.

"Almost, honey," Deborah said. "We'll just need to be careful, is all."

"I don't like it," Mr. Jang muttered, as they all gathered at the table and passed around the syrup and flapjacks. "It's not safe. Not worth the risk."

"What's not?" asked Professor Blunderbunn, dressed in a ridiculous pastel suit and speckled bow tie (one of Aunt Janie's brother's old suits, he said when he caught Deborah staring). "Is everything settled? Do you need a lift back into town?"

"The Secret's out," Mr. Jang continued. "They know. We can't stay."

Nadine looked up at him, panicked.

"But—" she began, casting a look toward Jack.

"You can't leave!" Jack said, through a mouthful of blueberry flapjacks. Deborah handed him a napkin as a few crumbs sprayed over his plate. Aunt Janie just smiled and asked if anyone would like some honey on theirs. "I mean— we just— Mom!"

Deborah threw up her hands. "I don't have any say in it, Jack!"

"Are you staying?" Mr. Jang said. He looked rumpled and tired, but his eyes crackled as he looked around the low table. A single flapjack was on his plate, dusted with cinnamon. "You know that's dangerous, Deb."

"Everywhere is dangerous for us," Deborah snapped. She sighed. "Truthfully, John, I'm not sure where we'd go. My sister is all the way in Kansas."

"Kansas?" cried Jack and Nadine simultaneously.

"I have an idea," Mr. Jang said quietly.

CHAPTER 32

And so we come to the end of the road. Jack and Nadine had, single-handedly, discovered the villain behind the destruction of the Magical Creature Reserve, and pieced together his plot to divide the Golden and Black Bloods. They had even saved a few lives, stopped the slaughter, brought the authorities around to arrest a few Fixers, and made the world safer for humanity and its misfits—at least for a little while.

Unfortunately, this was not gym class, so they received no ribbons or medals. Hardly anyone knew what they had done, and in this Crusty was correct: had people known who Jack's father was, I'm afraid they would have reacted a little less positively than they should have.

That is what you would call an understatement.

For you see, when you are the son of Death, your life is not all roses and butterflies. In fact, it does not contain any roses or butterflies. If you save the world—which Jack turned out to have quite the aptitude for—you don't get a thank you or an "atta boy." Most likely you will get a lecture and a demand for an explanation as to why Uncle Herman was snatched by your father before his time.

But I get ahead of myself.

CHAPTER 33

Here is what you need to know:

Professor Blunderbunn took a holiday, urging Mr. Jang and Ms. Hallows to get in touch with him, should they require anything. He said it mostly because he was quite certain he would never hear from them again.

Aunt Janie made them all flapjacks again for dinner, before they departed. She told Deborah that shortbread cookies were incredibly unhealthy, and asked if Deborah would not like some more butter with her flapjacks?

Crusty fled with a skeleton crew, those few who had managed to avoid arrest. They escaped to an old abandoned cookie factory, where they lived off of stale shortbreads and burnt macadamia nuts until they

161

received new orders—which, Crusty kept insisting, would soon be coming. Some of them believed him and stayed. Others looked at the stale shortbreads, the crispy-black nuts, and the dour factory, and decided that their convictions were not strong enough to make them eat subpar cookies. It is always, coincidentally, a good test of one's convictions.

Urkel and his family had to move to a new town. Ubork took the fall for the breached gate (quite unwillingly, I might add), and was forced to resign. That means he was fired.

Jack and Nadine did not go back into town, at least not for long. Mr. Jang's idea turned out to be quite a good one, and Deborah finally agreed. While Deborah went to spend some time with her sister in Kansas, and Mr. Jang moved to the city where his company's main offices were, Nadine and Jack were shipped off to boarding school.

Yes, they had exactly the same reaction.

The boarding school was called Magic Hallows and to describe it would take a great many more pages than we have here. But let us say that it was a boarding school that not just *anyone* could enter, nor was it one that just *anyone* would want to attend. Jack and Nadine, after they had time to adjust to the idea (and after they realized Magic Hallows was home to a world-famous pancake chef), were much more amenable to the proposition. That is to say, they quite liked it.

You see, it is always good to have friends when you go on new adventures. Especially friends who share big, grand Secrets. And especially *especially* friends with whom you have a very Secret alliance.

That, I thought, *will not be fun to explain to Death.*

About the Author

M.L. Windsor lives in Michigan, the only state with more Magical Creature reserves than zoos. A 2012 graduate of Harvard University, the author earned a degree in the History of Science, which is like magic without any of the nonsense. The Windsor pedigree boasts elves, giants, and one Norwegian troll, but the family prefers not to talk about him.

"It's not every day that your best friend gets eaten by a troll and the wall around the reserve containing gruesome magical creatures comes down unleashing evil on your town. Jack may be the son of Death but can he save the lives of friends and family before the Grim Reapers snatch up their souls? Windsor's debut middle-grade novel is full of twists and turns and secrets that keep you turning pages to find out how it all turns out in the end."

— Alyson Beecher, Kid Lit Frenzy

"Mix a pinch of *Percy Jackson,* a touch of the Baudelaire children, a tad of *Goosebumps,* an action-packed storyline with cliffhangers, humor, and a car chase, and a whole lot of rich vocabulary delivered in short chapters and you get an idea of what's bubblin' in *Jack Death.* The non-stop action and drama with great descriptive passages and derring-do will keep readers engaged as Jack and Nadine dash, dart, and dive, gulping great gasps of air to escape bullies, trolls, ogres, and just plain old bad guys. Like me, they'll be hooked and won't put it down!"

— Stephanie Bange, Director, Educational Resource Center, Wright State University

"*Jack Death* is a little bit Lemony Snicket, and a little bit of *The Munsters,* but with a lovable hero and unique concept that are all its own. Quirky, charming, and delightful to read, *Jack Death* is unlike any children's book I've read this year. I only hope that there's a sequel in the works!"

— Rebekah Hendrian, The Book Nook and Java Shop, Montague, Michigan